# CRADLE SNATCH

Mr Justice Craythorne is convinced that Janice Beaton is a wicked woman and sentences her to three years in prison — but later he is to discover just how wicked she is. After kidnapping the judge's baby grandson, she proceeds to terrorise his family . . . Cathy Weston leads the investigation but finds herself becoming emotionally involved with the baby's father. The physical and psychological pressures mount, and the young and vulnerable police inspector now finds herself targeted by Beaton and her sinister accomplice.

PETER CONWAY

# CRADLE SNATCH

*Complete and Unabridged*

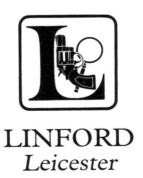

# LINFORD
*Leicester*

First published in Great Britain by
Robert Hale Limited
London

First Linford Edition
published 2006
by arrangement with
Robert Hale Limited
London

British Library CIP Data

Conway, Peter, *1903* –
   Cradle snatch.—Large print ed.—
Linford mystery library
   1. Kidnapping—Fiction
   2. Revenge—Fiction
   3. Policewomen—Fiction
   4. Detective and mystery stories
   5. Large type books
   I. Title
823.9′14 [F]

ISBN 1–84617–370–1

Published by
F. A. Thorpe (Publishing)
Anstey, Leicestershire

Set by Words & Graphics Ltd.
Anstey, Leicestershire
Printed and bound in Great Britain by
T. J. International Ltd., Padstow, Cornwall

This book is printed on acid-free paper

# 1

Janice Beaton lay on the narrow bed staring up at the ceiling; the day she had been waiting for impatiently for nearly three years was only a few short hours away. It had been hate, pure unadulterated hate that had kept her going through the long weary months; hate for the screws, hate for all those who had turned against her and above all, hate for the man who had put her away.

It was his summing up that had done it. It was not so much what he had said — he had been far too clever for that — but his facial expression and the tone of voice he had used when he said it. He had influenced the jury as surely as if he had told them outright to find her guilty. Conspiracy to pervert the course of justice indeed! What justice was it that had allowed her to go to prison and all the rest of them to get off scot-free? The man had also taken a sadistic delight in sentencing her; she had been over the scene so many times in her mind that she was able to remember it all as if it were yesterday.

There had been an expectant hush in the crowded court-room as the judge cleared his throat, put the tips of his long thin fingers together and levelled his gaze at the young woman standing in the dock.

'Janice Mary Beaton,' he said, his high-pitched voice reaching to every corner of the room, 'you have been found guilty of a very serious offence by the jury after a trial lasting for ten days. Having heard all the evidence about your activities, I have come to the conclusion that you are a thoroughly wicked woman and I am bound to say that I agree entirely with their verdict. I have listened very carefully to what your Counsel had to say on your behalf, but the fact remains that your corruption of witnesses has been a quite deliberate course of conduct and I would be failing in my duty if I did not send you to prison for a long time. The public must be protected from people such as you and in the circumstances, the least sentence I can pass on you is three years in prison.'

Janice Beaton stood there staring at the judge for a full minute and then turned to face the crowded benches; not a single one of the men and women who had given evidence against her was able to meet her gaze and her lips twisted in a contemptuous smile. Before leaving the dock and going down the steps, she faced Judge Craythorne once more and gave him a look of such concentrated malignancy, that even with his experience, he was unable to suppress the feelings of anxiety and unease that were to remain with him for several days.

'Of course we'll appeal, I'll . . .'

'Three years!' Janice's harsh voice cut off the solicitor abruptly in mid-sentence. 'You told me I'd get off with a fine; I'd have done a bloody sight better to have pleaded guilty. You and that idiot Morris have cost me a fortune and look where it's got me. For the last ten days, I've been insulted and humiliated and all you can do is bleat at me: 'of course we'll appeal.' You know as well as I do that it'll be a complete waste of time and where the hell do you think the money's coming from? You bloody well make me sick and I never want to see you again. Get out!'

The man shrugged his shoulders and stalked out of the cell. Janice managed to keep control over herself until the door shut behind him, then threw herself on to the ground, sobbing bitterly and pounding the floor with her fists.

★   ★   ★

For the first six months, Janice was overcome by a deep depression. She was twenty-six and for the preceding five years had known nothing but the heights of luxury; only the very best had been good enough for her and she had enough money to indulge every whim, food, clothes, jewellery and holidays in exotic places. Starting with her drunken father, she had always despised men and her days as a call-girl had done nothing to change that view. As soon as she had enough money put by, she started to get things organized and the running of her own show proved not only more lucrative, but much more emotionally rewarding too; power and the ability to make the puppets dance on her string was what she found so satisfying.

Now, there were only the rough clothes, the menial work and the harsh commands of the hated screws; it was almost more than she could bear and if she had been less depressed and had more energy, she might well have done something to finish it all for good. She wandered around as if in a dream, ignoring the others, obeying orders mechanically and saying almost nothing. She lost weight, her face took on a ghostly pallor and although for a time one or two of the other prisoners tried to cheer her up, they soon gave up when there was no response and left her to her own devices.

Janice realized later that what had saved her sanity was an incident that occurred in the workroom one day. She had been sitting at the long wooden table mechanically sewing an overall, when the insistent whimpering of the girl next to her penetrated the barrier of her misery. She looked up; Cynthia, a large coarse featured woman, an epileptic of uncertain temper and considerable strength, was crushing the hand of the other girl in her enormous fist.

Janice got to her feet without conscious thought. 'Let her go,' she said, hardly raising her voice.

Cynthia merely grinned and tightened her grip, provoking an anguished cry from her victim.

'Belt up Janice, unless of course you'd like some of the same treatment yourself.'

Janice picked up the heavy cutting-out shears by the blades and hit the woman as hard as she could across the mouth with the metal handles. Cynthia's head jerked back with the sudden shock of the blow, her hand went to her mouth and she looked uncomprehendingly at the broken tooth and the blood, which was by now streaming down her chin. Quite suddenly her expression of consternation changed to one of horror and she half rose to her feet; for a moment there was complete silence and then an unearthly scream burst from the woman's chest. She collapsed into her chair and as her spine arched like a bow, it fell over backwards with a tremendous crash. Twisting and writhing, the woman went into a series of violent convulsions and then lay as if dead, blood coursing from her mouth.

'All right, all right! Back to your seats everyone.'

Two of the officers came running up and a few minutes later, calm was restored.

'She just had a fit, see?'

Janice looked round at the others and then smiled for the first time for weeks. She had seen expressions like those of the girls nearby before — things were going to be a lot different now. From that time on Janice's attitude changed completely; she realized that with full remission, she would only have just over eighteen more months to serve and that was not really such a long time — she would still be under thirty when she came out and there would be nothing to stop her getting organized again.

Janice had also discovered something

else — she enjoyed hurting people. When she had hit Cynthia, she had experienced an intense feeling of power and satisfaction that was almost sensuous in its quality and the fact that the others were now afraid of her made it all the better. Once fully out of her depression, Janice also discovered that there were many ways of making life easier for herself.

It soon became obvious that some of the prison officers were not immune to certain suggestions and by exerting herself in that direction, she managed to get herself put into the same room as Rita Channing, the one girl who both attracted her and would make a congenial companion. Rita was a pretty, fluffy, blonde girl, who had got herself involved in an attempt to blackmail an MP; secretly Janice thought her vain and stupid, but she was good looking, even tempered and above all quite prepared to go along with whatever the older woman suggested.

Despite her newly found sense of purpose, the time passed slowly, particularly after Rita had been released and that last night seemed never ending. Janice was too tensed up and excited to sleep and the constant snivelling of the girl in the other bed was getting on her nerves. Sandra Wilson had only been in the room with her for a fortnight and in that time had hardly stopped crying for more than a few minutes. She was only doing nine months, but had had a miscarriage soon after her arrival and since then had been inconsolable. If it hadn't meant risking the loss of her remission, Janice would have given her something worth crying about long since, but with only a week or two to go, she was determined to keep a tight control over her temper.

When at last Sandra did fall asleep, light was already beginning to filter in through the curtains and Janice could feel the nervous anticipation beginning to creep up on her — it wouldn't be long now. She was proposing to give it a reasonable time — say six months — and then Mr Justice Craythorne would get what he so richly deserved.

★   ★   ★

'Good luck.'

Janice Beaton didn't even bother to look round at the woman who had spoken to her and who was holding open the side door of the prison; she pushed past and walked straight out into the drizzle.

'Look this way please Miss Beaton.'

The shock of seeing the group of reporters and newsmen was too much for her, it was all so totally unexpected, and she stood there looking round like a hunted animal as the flash bulbs went off.

'What's it feel like to be free again?'

'What are you going to do now?'

'A nice big smile please Miss Beaton.'

For a moment, Janice nearly gave way to complete panic — a lot of publicity was something she could do without. She suddenly caught sight of the unmistakable figure of Randolph Naughton standing a short distance away from the others and had a sudden flash of inspiration. Naughton was the one reporter who had been sympathetic towards her when reporting the trial and once or twice had even smiled at her when she had been in the witness box.

She elbowed her way towards him. 'Can you get me out of this?'

The man gave a half smile and nodded, ushering her towards a waiting taxi.

'How much do you want for your story?' he asked when they were well away from the prison.

'How much are you prepared to offer?'

He named a figure that almost shook her resolve.

'Take me to a decent hotel, let me have a bath, give me breakfast and I'll think about it.'

An hour later, Naughton sipped a cup of black coffee and watched the woman across the table through the smoke of his cigarette — this was going to be a scoop worth having. He had written his piece at the time of the trial with this eventuality very much in mind and it looked now as if his hunch was going to pay off, but at all costs he had to prevent any of the others from getting anywhere near her.

Janice ate her way slowly through a large plate of scrambled eggs and had just started on her third piece of toast and marmalade, when she suddenly put one hand to her stomach and the other to her mouth.

'I'm sorry,' she said in a weak voice, 'it's the first decent meal I've had in more than two years and . . . ' She doubled up and made a dash for the door.

Even though she had left her coat over the back of the chair, Naughton followed her out after a moment or two. The ladies' cloakroom was on one side of the foyer and he leaned against a pillar, keeping the door in sight. An opportunity like this only came up once or twice in a career and he wasn't going to run the risk of having her walk out on him. He waited for ten minutes and then went up to the reception desk.

'Can I help you sir?'

'Yes, the young lady I was with was taken ill a few minutes ago and I wondered if you would go into the cloakroom to see if she's all right.'

'Of course sir.'

Even before she spoke, one look at the girl's expression when she came out again was enough to confirm his worst fears.

'There's no one in there at all.'

'Are you quite sure?'

'Absolutely sir.'

'Did you see her come out of the dining-room about ten minutes ago — a dark girl wearing a white blouse and a grey skirt?'

'A lady of that description did go out of the front entrance — I noticed her particularly as she seemed to be in rather a hurry.'

★　★　★

Outwitting the reporter had done wonders for Janice Beaton's morale, but a week later it was standing even higher. She had recovered the £5,000 in cash and most of her jewellery, which she had put in a safe deposit long before her arrest, had had her hair dyed and restyled, bought herself some new clothes — her own were pathetically out of fashion — and rented a furnished flat. She was appalled at the cost of everything, particularly the flat and the second-hand car which she decided she could not do without, but for the time being, she didn't care how much she spent and it was essential for her to have a safe base from which to work.

Once, too, she had discovered that Craythorne was still alive and kicking — it had been a constant anxiety to her that he might have died while she was in Holloway — she began to relax. At this stage, she had no intention of hurrying; she was quite prepared to wait the full six months she had decided on in prison and knew perfectly well that if she took action too quickly after her release, the police would be bound to suspect her straight away. As yet, she had no clear idea of exactly what she was going to do to him, but there would be plenty of time to think about that later.

It took Janice several weeks to adjust to being on her own, free from the constant noise and chatter which had been such a feature of prison life. At times she felt intensely lonely, but she most certainly was not going to contact any of her former associates or family, who in any case had long since made it quite clear that they wanted nothing further to do with her. Gradually, the colour came back into her cheeks, even her hands, which she thought had been permanently ruined by all the hard work and the coarse soap, were beginning to show signs of recovery. Finally, a fortnight by the seaside, enjoying such simple pleasures as sitting in the sun, walking along the sands and going to the cinema, completed her rehabilitation.

Waiting for the day exactly six months from the date of her release added to the pleasurable anticipation and when she walked into the public library and took *Who's Who* down from the shelf, her hands were shaking so much that she could hardly turn the pages. Janice let out a deep sigh of released tension when she saw the entry and read out the heading slowly to herself.

''CRAYTHORNE, Hon. Sir Arthur, Kt. 1967; Hon. Mr Justice Craythorne.''

She copied out the complete section and sat there for a while, a frown of concentration on her face. It was a good enough start all right; the man was a widower, he had one daughter and his private address in London was there. But what next? Five minutes later she had made up her mind. No doubt an enquiry agent would be able to provide her with all the information she needed, but it would be so much more satisfying to do it all herself; it would be an added challenge and much safer too.

# 2

The faded-looking woman wearing a felt hat and a plastic mackintosh had been trying unsuccessfully to give her religious pamphlets to the passers-by in Oxford Street ever since the shops had opened. It was a Saturday morning, a light rain was falling and the people seemed even less interested than usual. After having been pushed and jostled for a good hour and a half, she retreated to the relative haven of the entrance to a disused shop and approached the four people who were sheltering there waiting for a bus. When they saw her walking towards them, as if by a prearranged signal, they all turned away to study the empty display area with intense concentration, except for a smartly dressed woman in her late twenties, who not only stood her ground, but stared at her in a way that made her blush nervously behind her spectacles.

'Can I interest you in . . . ' she began

timidly, holding out one of the damp pamphlets.

'Yes, you certainly can,' the woman replied after studying it for some time. 'Can you spare me several? I would like to give them to my friends.'

'How many would you like?'

Miss Trimble handed over half the pile and watched the woman out of sight with tears of joy welling up in her pale blue eyes. It was rare moments such as this that made the struggle worth while. She settled her hat more firmly on her head and strode purposefully back into the milling throng on the pavement.

★　★　★

Even though Janice Beaton knew that there was no real risk of Judge Craythorne recognizing her, her heart was still thumping painfully in her chest as she rang the bell of the mews cottage in Knights-bridge. She could have wept with disappointment when a middle-aged woman opened the door and promptly started to close it again directly she saw the pamphlets in her hand.

'Who is it Mrs Davies?'

The man who came into the hall and opened the door more widely was undoubtedly Judge Craythorne — Janice had found a photograph of him in one of the morning papers a few weeks earlier — but without his robes and wig, he looked so unlike the stern figure in court whom she remembered so vividly, that she could only stare at him in astonishment. He was a short man, wearing a crumpled sports jacket with leather insets at the elbows, a pair of baggy grey flannel trousers and had some very antique carpet slippers on his feet. He gave her a warm smile and held out his hand to take the proferred leaflet.

'I don't belong to your church, but I'd be glad to study this. Good morning.'

The man had looked so utterly inoffensive that it was not until she had got back to her flat that she really got down to the serious business of thinking up methods of paying him back for the way in which he had made her suffer. Everything she considered seemed to

19

have at least one major snag to it and it was not until the following afternoon that it became clear to her what she had to do.

Earlier that day, she sat in her estate-car parked within sight of the Judge's house and when he came out soon after mid-day and set off down the street, she started the engine and began to go after him. There was hardly any traffic about, she had no trouble with one-way streets and when she saw him ring the bell of the house in a road just off Cadogan Square, she was quite certain that he had no suspicion that he had been followed. She parked right opposite the house, which was the end one in the terrace and was tall and narrow, having five stories in addition to the basement.

After a time, when it was quite clear that the Judge was staying for lunch, she walked past it and round the corner into the next street. As she had expected, there was no rear entrance and she went back to the car and settled down to wait.

It was soon after two o'clock when the front door came open and a very large young man in his early twenties wheeled a pram down the three stone steps, waited until Craythorne had joined him and then put his head back inside.

'Sure you'll be all right?' he shouted. Janice was unable to hear the reply. 'O.K. then, we'll be back in good time for tea. 'Bye.'

The young man slammed the door and the two of them went off in the direction of Hyde Park. For some twenty minutes they walked along without talking and then, when the baby had gone off to sleep, they sat down on one of a pair of benches which were standing back to back. The opportunity was too good to miss; Janice made a wide detour and sat down behind them, opening out her newspaper.

'I'm afraid that the last year hasn't been much fun for you, John,' Craythorne said when he had got his pipe going.

'No, that's true but Mary does seem to be picking up a bit now and the doctors always did warn me that these post child-birth depressions can take a very long time to clear up completely. It's something that she's beginning to feel like

21

doing things for Mark at last and it's a great consolation that at least he's fighting fit.'

'Yes, you must be very proud of him, I know I am. There's nothing quite like the first grandchild, you know; being able to see him every Sunday's taken years off me.'

Janice had heard enough. As she walked back to the car, she realized that the situation was just waiting to be exploited; she hadn't begun to work out the details yet, but she knew with utter certainty that somehow she was going to kidnap that baby. None of the other ideas she had had could touch it for its simplicity and the sureness with which it would break up the high and mighty Mr Justice Craythorne. The fact that his daughter was obviously still recovering from a nervous breakdown would make it all the more devastating. The possibilities seemed endless.

In the course of the next week, Janice spent many hours patiently watching the house in Chelsea and gradually began to build up a picture of the set-up. The basement was occupied by a middle-aged couple. Janice followed the man one morning and discovered that he worked as a porter in one of the large department stores in Knightsbridge; the woman was obviously the housekeeper, as not only did she pass in front of various windows in the house during the course of the day, but she opened the front door to tradesmen and when she went to the local grocer one morning, Janice heard her ask the man to put the order down to Mrs Livingstone's account.

Every morning, promptly at eight fifteen, the young man she had overheard talking to the judge in the park stroked the large black cat, which was always sitting on the front steps, let it in through the front door and then strode off down the road. Janice followed him on one occasion; the man in the dark suit, wearing a bowler hat and carrying a brief-case and a furled umbrella, was six foot three inches tall and went along at such a pace that she kept on having to break into a trot to keep up with him.

It was a warm morning, she was out of

condition and her shoes were not designed for running. By the time he had crossed Piccadilly and arrived at his office, she was utterly exhausted and had a blister the size of a 10p piece on the back of her right heel. She comforted herself, however, with the thought that she had at least found out both where he worked and what he did, as by the side of the door was a large brass plate, which read:

LIVINGSTONE AND CO
SOLICITORS AND COMMISSIONERS
FOR OATHS

Janice also very soon found out that the Livingstones were obviously doing very nicely indeed. In addition to the house, which in that part of London must have cost a fortune, and the housekeeper, there was a resident nanny, who had charge of the baby during the day.

Following her presented no difficulties; every day, if the weather was fine, she took the baby out in the pram. In the mornings, she usually went into the private garden in Cadogan Square and allowed him to kick about on a rug on the grass and in the afternoons, she wheeled him up to Hyde Park. The nanny appeared to be in her early sixties, was obviously getting a bit short of breath and spoke with a strong Scottish accent.

Even though she hated all babies and this one in particular, Janice had to admit that he was a fine looking boy, with the same fair hair and blue eyes as his father and he clearly had an equable temperament, being placid and contented. As for Mrs Livingstone, Janice never once saw her leave the house; on one or two occasions a figure crossed in front of one of the windows, but that was all.

★   ★   ★

Janice spent many hours considering various plans and it was obvious to her, long before she came up with the final version, that she was going to need help. It was not her intention to kill the baby, at least not straight away, and in that case, if she did manage to snatch him someone was going to have to look after him and that someone was not going to be her; not only did she dislike babies intensely, but she would need complete freedom of action if her ideas were going to work out.

At first, it seemed as if her plans might founder at the first hurdle. She had no relatives of her own whom she could employ and while it was true that she had made plenty of contacts in Holloway, there was no one she could think of who might be trusted to cope. In fact, the only person she had got to know really well was Rita Channing, but the idea of her either wanting or for that matter being able to deal with a baby was laughable. Apart from that, the girl was too soft-hearted and scatter-brained to be entirely trustworthy.

It was while she was thinking about Rita and re-living some of the things they had done together, that the idea of Sandra Wilson suddenly came into her head. Janice remembered that her release date was only a week away — like all the others she had talked of little else — and decided to meet her outside the prison.

The more she thought about it, the more promising a person Sandra seemed to be; the girl would be bound to need the money, she was crazy about children and above all, would do exactly what she was told. Sandra wasn't very bright and Janice felt quite confident of her ability to make up a suitable tale to tell her. The thought of having the baby in her flat didn't exactly enchant her, but if it meant the success of her plans it would be well worth it.

Janice also urgently needed help and advice over the rest of her plans and Rita Channing was the obvious person, particularly with her experience, albeit unsuccessful, of blackmail. She ran her to earth in the club where she was working and during the lunch hour they walked up the road to Soho Square and sat on one of the benches in the central garden. After they had chatted for a few minutes, Rita looked across knowingly at her friend.

'I don't suppose you brought me here just to tell me about your new flat — what's up Janice?'

'I'm running a bit short of money and there's someone who needs to be taught a lesson. I thought I'd kill two birds with one stone and I've worked out a way of putting the black on him; that's where you come in — I want your advice about the best way to collect the money.'

Rita giggled. 'I'm hardly the best person to come to — look where it landed me.' She thought for a few moments before continuing, her forehead furrowed with concentration. 'It's more tricky than you might think; unless you're dealing with someone like a bookie or a club owner, you can't expect people to be able to lay their hands on large sums of money without giving them a bit of notice, and that gives them time to think it all over. The police are always very much on the side of the so-called victims, however much they deserve what's coming to them, and that's how one can so easily get caught — it's not difficult for them to set up a trap.'

'I realize that and that's why I wanted your views on how to set about it.'

'How much were you thinking of taking him for?'

'£20,000 as a start — not too little and not too much. I've been finding out about him in the last week or two and I reckon he's quite capable of finding that sort of money.'

'What have you got on him? Do you think he'll pay?'

'He'll pay all right. No offence Rita, but I wasn't proposing to tell anyone about the details.'

'That'll make it much more difficult, you know. If I find someone to do the collecting for you, they'll want to know what the risks are, otherwise they won't touch it and if you don't tell me, how can you expect me to know who to approach?'

Janice thought for a long time before replying. 'All right then, it looks as if I haven't got much choice — I was thinking of snatching a baby.'

Rita let out a low whistle. 'That's going to come a bit expensive.'

'Why ever should it? I was proposing to take the baby myself.'

'The police like kidnappers even less than blackmailers and collecting the money's always the most difficult part. I do know one man who might be prepared to take it on.'

'Would your bloke also be prepared to arrange for the mother to be roughed up a bit later on?'

'Exactly what did you have in mind?'

'I want her fixed so that she'll never be able to look in a mirror again without shuddering, fixed so that no plastic surgeon would ever be able to repair the damage. I want her to remain conscious throughout and finally, I intend to be there to watch it all and I have certain ideas of my own.'

Janice was breathing heavily and Rita was appalled by the vicious expression on her face. 'Mr Grey might be able to help you,' she said, after a long pause.

'Who's he?'

'Runs the club where I work, amongst other things. If you do see him though, you'll go easy, won't you?'

'What are you talking about Rita? You didn't used to be so windy.'

'He can be very touchy can Mr Grey.'

'So can I. When can you arrange for me to meet him?'

'Now, if you like. He was in the club when I left.'

'Very well, that'll suit me fine. Now listen Rita, I don't want him to know my name, where I live, nor what I really look like. Is there a place near here where I can buy a wig?'

'No problem.'

'And Rita, you will keep this to yourself, won't you?'

'What do you think I am?'

'I know I can trust you all right, but I've had enough of trusting other people and I don't want any slip-ups.'

'I hope to God you know what you're doing.'

'I know what I'm doing all right.'

'Well, I won't say anything, I can promise you that.'

'Thanks Rita, I knew I could bank on you. There'll be a hundred in it for you too, if you give me a bit of a hand.'

★　★　★

Six days later, Janice was pacing up and down outside the entrance to the prison, waiting impatiently for Sandra Wilson to come out. The preliminaries had taken her longer than she had expected and she was getting progressively more tense as time went by. She was getting through money at an alarming rate and the advance that Grey had required for the two jobs had made a large dent in her reserves.

The minute that Janice had seen Grey, she realised why Rita had warned her about him — in a quiet way, he terrified her too. In the first place, there had been his appearance. She was not sure exactly what sort of person she had been expecting, but it was not the slim, pale young man in the immaculate clothes, who had stared at her disdainfully across the table at the club. Then, too, there had been his accent; he said no more than two dozen words to her and yet those clipped tones made her forget she was trying to buy his services. The casual authority of the upper classes was something she had hated all her life and yet she was almost hypnotized into agreeing to the man's outrageous terms.

'Take it or leave it,' he had said shortly when she started to protest. 'I'll give you five minutes to decide; after that, it's off.'

She had opened her mouth to speak again, but after one look at those snake-like eyes, she hurriedly changed her mind. At least, she thought, after she had left the club, the job would be done both ruthlessly and efficiently.

Three days later, when she came back with the money, he tossed it disdainfully across to one of his men and while it was counted out, stared at her unblinkingly until she was forced to look away and shifted uncomfortably in her chair.

'Now listen carefully,' he said when the man had finished, 'I will arrange for the money to be collected for you today week, next Thursday, and exactly three days after that we will attend to that other matter — you will have to fit your own plans into that timetable. Now this is what I propose . . . '

For the next ten minutes he spoke quietly and with complete confidence and authority and for the first time, Janice lost all her doubts about the feasibility of the plan.

'Although we may be able to scare them into keeping the police out of it, I am not banking on it and will be assuming that they will try to set a sophisticated trap, despite any warnings that we give. All the same, I think my plan should cover every eventuality. I gather that you want this woman to suffer as much as possible, is that right?' Janice nodded. 'Well, there is one little refinement that might commend itself to you, but it will cost you a bit extra.'

'What is it?' As Janice listened, she could not prevent herself from smiling, despite her nervousness. 'I had a somewhat similar idea myself — the two will go together quite admirably.'

'Any other questions?'

'How will I give you the rest of the money?'

'My assistant will collect it from you when the second part of the operation has been completed to your satisfaction.'

'Will you be there yourself?'

'I am not in the habit of being questioned about my personal arrangements. I wish you a good afternoon.'

'There was one last thing.'

Grey looked up. 'Oh, and what's that?'

'I want to buy a gun.'

Janice saw him purse his thin lips together more firmly. 'Why?'

'I am not in the habit of being questioned about my personal arrangements.'

Janice could feel the perspiration running down the inside of her dress as she tried to meet his gaze steadily. For perhaps ten seconds he stared at her, then the merest hint of a smile flitted across his pale face.

'Mulligan! See to it for her.'

Janice didn't know how she had managed to find the courage to speak to him like that, but it had certainly paid dividends as far as his two underlings were concerned; she sensed at once that they were treating her with new respect and she even managed to get the gun for a reasonable price.

★   ★   ★

Janice was just beginning to get anxious when in the distance she heard the rattle of keys, the side door opened and Sandra Wilson appeared. She let her get well clear of the prison and then came up behind her.

'Hello Sandra. I thought I'd welcome you out.'

The girl stared at her, unable to believe her eyes and then burst into tears, flinging her arms round the other woman's neck. Janice just held her for a moment without speaking.

'Nowhere to go?' Sandra shook her head miserably. 'Come to my place and we'll think of something.'

The young woman didn't say anything until they were inside the flat. She was so depressed that she didn't seem to see anything strange in the fact that the other woman both had a car and an expensive flat. She revived a little after having eaten some breakfast, but even so, Janice decided not to frighten her by rushing things.

'Don't you have any relatives?' she asked.

'Well, there is my mum — she's a widow and lives in Bristol — but she doesn't know that I've been inside. She'd have me back, I know she would, but she hasn't got much money and in any case, I left because it was so boring. I don't know what to do — if only I hadn't lost my baby.' She covered her face with her hands and began to sob quietly.

Janice left her there while she washed up the breakfast things and when she came back, Sandra had stopped crying and was sitting staring miserably out of the window.

'Cheer up,' she said, 'and I'll tell you the real reason why I brought you here. I was asked to help out a friend the other day and I thought immediately that it might be just the thing for you, right up your street in fact, and the pay'll be quite good as well. You see, I used to work for Max Fennell before he got killed in a road accident; he was a bit before your time, but he used to manage a lot of pop groups. He was the one who discovered 'The Giraffes' you know.' Janice saw that the other girl's interest was beginning to quicken. 'As you can imagine, I know the members of the group pretty well and when I got out, I was lucky enough to get a job with them. Now you won't tell a soul about this, will you?' Sandra shook her head. 'Well, Pauline — she's the lead singer, you know — had a baby about a year ago. It's been kept a secret — she thought the fans wouldn't like it — and she gave me the job of finding someone to look after him while the group's in America. They leave on Monday — I expect you read about it. Pauline did make other arrangements, of course, but they fell through only yesterday; we were at our wits' end to know what to do, but then I thought of you. You will help me, won't you Sandra? They've got pots of money these pop stars and you'll get expenses plus twenty quid a week.'

'Do you think I could manage it?'

'Of course you could. You know how much you love babies and how good you are with them.' Janice had a sudden thought. 'Why not take him up to stay with your mum? I'm afraid that she mustn't be in the secret, but I could drive you up and pretend to be a social worker or something. We could say that the baby's mother was having a serious operation and we were employing you to look after him until other arrangements were made.'

Janice could see that Sandra was beginning to get excited about the idea and knew that she had won. With any luck, Mrs Wilson would be as dumb as her daughter and swallow the story just as easily.

'He'll have clothes and everything won't he?'

'Yes, of course he will, but Pauline had what I thought was rather a good idea. I told her about you losing your baby and she thought it would be nice if you bought him some new things yourself — actually she gave me twenty-five quid for you to spend on them.'

'When will I have to start?'

'I hope to bring him round on Monday morning; that'll give you tomorrow and the day after to get the clothes. Perhaps we could drive up to you mum's place in the afternoon. Is she on the phone?'

'Yes she is, but I can't remember the number.' Sandra intercepted Janice's look of exasperation and a tear ran down her cheek. 'I'm sorry, but you see it's such a long time since I was at home.'

'Never mind. Let me have the address and I'll get it from directory enquiries; you can give her a ring tonight.'

Janice found the number without any difficulty, wrote it down on a scrap of paper and put it behind the mirror in her handbag with a sigh of satisfaction — yet another hurdle was over.

\* \* \*

The following Monday morning, Janice was waiting in her estate car parked at a meter on the side of the road opposite to the Livingstones' house. As soon as she saw movements behind the windows, she switched off the radio and screwed her eyes up with concentration. She had only to wait for fifteen minutes before she saw the large young man come out of the front door. As he walked down the steps on to the pavement, Janice thought in a moment of panic that he was going to come across to the car, but then she relaxed and smiled to herself as he looked around in every direction and whistled loudly a few times. Janice saw him purse his lips and shrug his shoulders briefly, then he picked up the three milk bottles and closed the front door behind him.

Janice's time-table was so tight that she could only afford at most a twenty-four hour delay and her relief when the day started fine and clear, was considerable. She waited patiently until Livingstone had left for work and felt the tension beginning to build up inside her.

Whenever Janice had been watching, the nanny had always left the house a few minutes on either side of ten o'clock. This morning was no exception and the elderly woman walked slowly towards the garden in the square a quarter of a mile away. As she fiddled with the lock on the gate, Janice strolled towards the pram and inspected it as carefully as she could. She now saw that in comparison with the one of the same make and colour that she had been able to buy on the previous

Saturday, it had faded quite badly and there were spots of rust on the chrome; nevertheless she was satisfied that the new one would pass a casual inspection.

After she had telephoned Rita at the club to fix a meeting place, there was nothing further to be done and she returned to the flat. The next couple of hours seemed an eternity, but at last the time came for her to leave. She picked up Rita without incident and at half past one they were parked in sight of the Livingstones' house.

'It'll be as easy as falling off a log; I don't know what you're in such a state about, I'm the one who should be nervous.'

'There's something I don't like about this job Janice.'

'Perhaps this'll make you feel better about it.' She held up the wad of fivers for the other woman to see. 'Meet me back at the car when I've got him and they're yours.'

'I don't know, I . . . '

'Here she comes.'

They watched as the old nanny wheeled the pram carefully down the steps and began to walk slowly towards Sloane Street. Janice started the car and drove off in the opposite direction.

'Where are you going?'

'Just to find a meter near the park. That old woman had taken the same route every time I've followed her so far; don't worry, she's obviously a creature of habit, we won't miss her.'

Five minutes later, the two women unloaded the collapsible pram from the back of the estate car and carefully reassembled it.

'What's the second pram in the back for?'

'The baby, of course. You didn't think I'd keep this one, did you? It'll be dynamite. Now, have you got it all straight?'

'Yes, I think so.'

'Let's go over it all again once more as we walk along.'

\* \* \*

Ethel Robertson leaned forward and gripped the baby's foot, giving it a gentle shake. The little boy gave a shriek of delight and waved his arms about wildly, making the row of plastic balls, which were strung across the pram, rattle violently.

'Oh, but you're a dear wee thing,' she said, smiling down happily at the fair haired baby.

Six months earlier, Ethel Robertson had never dreamed that she would be able to work again. With her arthritic knee, she was not so quick about the place as she used to be and she was the first to admit that her memory was beginning to go. She had applied for the job without any real expectation of getting it and had almost resigned herself to retirement and going to live with her sister in Streatham.

Within five minutes of meeting her, John Livingstone had had no doubt at all that the elderly Scotswoman was just the person he was looking for. Slow she may have been, but she was clearly experienced, reliable and above all kindly. For her part, once she had got over her astonishment at being appointed, Miss

Robertson could not have been more delighted with her position. She liked John Livingstone, who did not fuss her, she got on well with the housekeeper and her husband and the baby was the apple of her eye. As for Mrs Livingstone, the poor woman hardly ever said a word and spent most of the day lying in bed.

By the time she had reached her favourite seat in the park, the baby was fast asleep, lolling forward against the straps. She settled him back, arranged the pram so that the sun was off his face and sat back with a little sigh of pleasure; the trees were just beginning to turn and as usual, she looked around her, savouring the familiar sights and sounds of the park.

At that time in the afternoon, that particular area was practically deserted and she idly watched the young woman who was walking slowly in front of her some fifty yards away. Although the old lady couldn't see all that clearly, it was obvious that the girl was having some difficulty in negotiating the rough ground in her ludicrous high heels. Miss Robertson had little sympathy for her; she didn't approve of shoes like that, but at least she was dressed like a woman. The old nanny had no patience with the clothes that young people seemed to wear nowadays; in her young day, men were men and women were women and no nonsense about it.

She had just turned her head to watch a horseman in the distance, when the girl gave a cry and fell to the ground. Miss Robertson would have gone to her aid in any case, but she was in fact the only person in the vicinity and she hurried across as fast as her knee would allow. The young woman was sitting on the grass, clutching her ankle and her face was screwed up in pain.

'Have you hurt yourself then?'

'I think I've twisted my ankle.'

'Let me have a look at it. The ground here is awful treacherous with those shoes, isn't it?' She pressed firmly over the bone on the outer side of the girl's ankle and moved her foot about. 'Does that hurt?'

'Only a little.'

'Good, I don't think it's too bad. Now,

take my hand and we'll see if you can walk a wee bit.'

Now that she was close to, Miss Robertson could see that the young woman was just the sort of person of whom she most strongly disapproved. She was heavily made up, her jewellery was vulgar and it was only too obvious that she wasn't wearing anything under her thin blouse. Miss Robertson was a good-hearted soul, though, and none of her distaste showed on her face as she took the girl's arm.

'It might be a good thing for you to stick to the paths. There now, is it paining you less?'

'Yes, it's much better now. Thank you for your help — it was kind of you to come across.'

'Think nothing of it. Good-bye just now.'

All the hurrying and bending had stirred up the old lady's knee and she picked her way carefully back to the bench without looking behind her. If she had done so, she would have been astonished to see the young woman hurrying away, almost running and without the trace of a limp.

When she was still a few yards away, Miss Robertson sensed that something was wrong; perhaps it was the fact that the pram looked in some way strange, or that the hood was set at a different angle, but one glance inside made the blood drain from her face. The rattle was not there, the blanket was different and when she frantically snatched it away, all she saw was a pile of screwed up newspapers.

The old lady collasped back on the bench, unable to take it all in, feeling sick and faint with shock, an appalling tightness gripping her throat. A few moments later, she struggled to her feet and began to search desperately around the nearby trees, even though she knew it would be a complete waste of time, then broke into a travesty of a run when she saw a middle-aged man approaching.

'The baby! The baby!'

She was in a state of near prostration by the time he had hurried up and it was some minutes before he could get a coherent story out of her, but after he had taken a look inside the pram, he sat her firmly down on the bench.

'You stay here, my dear. I know it's been a great shock, but you mustn't move until I've found a policeman.' He gripped her hand and gave it a comforting squeeze. 'They'll soon get your baby back, you'll see.'

\*   \*   \*

When she got back to the car, Janice was bathed in perspiration and she was shaking so much that she could hardly get the key into the car door. By the time that Rita had appeared, though, she had got a firm grip on herself once more.

'I told you there'd be nothing to it.'

'I must hand it to you Janice, I didn't think it would be that easy. I'll be pushing off then.'

'O.K. Rita, here's your money, but before you go, give me a hand with the baby, will you? I want all his clothes changed — everything, including his nappy. I've got a spare set in the other pram.'

They were both clumsy, the baby had been woken suddenly and sensed at once that they were strangers; within minutes, he was screaming the place down and didn't stop until he had been strapped into the other pram and the car was on the move again.

On her way back to the tube station, Rita wheeled the Livingstones' pram, with all the clothes rolled up in a bundle inside, to one of the side entrances of a big department store, applied the brake and then walked inside. She only really felt safe when she had left by another entrance, had taken off the ridiculous gloves that Janice had insisted she wore the whole time, and was on her way back to the club.

⋆   ⋆   ⋆

Janice only managed to prevent herself from hitting the baby by the exercise of all her self control. Dyeing his hair and eyebrows proved more difficult than the whole of the rest of the exercise; he kicked and screamed and in her rubber gloves, she was clumsy. In the end, she managed it and although some of the dye had gone on to his forehead and scalp, it was at least gratifying to see what a difference it had made to his appearance and she had managed to avoid spilling any of it on his clothes.

The motion of the car seemed to be the one thing that quietened him down and by the time she had got back to her flat half an hour later, he had stopped crying and his hair was dry. She threw away the old piece of sheet with which the pillow had been protected and picked him up to take him inside; almost at once he began at first to whimper and then to bellow and she felt a stab of annoyance, tinged with envy, when he stopped the minute she handed him over to Sandra.

'What a lovely little boy!' Sandra chucked him under the chin and he gave a little gurgle of pleasure and began to play with her necklace. 'What's his name Janice?'

'Joe.'

Sandra's expression became quite transformed once she saw the baby; gone was the woebegone look and she became much more animated and lively.

'Hasn't he got beautiful blue eyes? It's funny with his black hair, isn't it, but perhaps they'll change colour later. Have I got time to give him a drink before we go?'

'Yes, but you won't take too long, will you? I want to get out of London before the rush hour.'

★   ★   ★

Four hours later, Janice drove back down the motorway from Bristol, exhausted from the effects of the long spell of nervous tension, but at the same time relieved at the thought that the most difficult part was over and that now she would be able to sit back and enjoy the fruits of all her planning and hard work.

To Janice's surprise, Sandra's mother must have been all of sixty. She was a thin, defeated looking woman, who was obviously a bit slow on the uptake. Janice gathered that she did a cleaning job, part time, to augment her widow's pension and it was obvious that she was delighted to have her daughter back at home and what's more, able to supplement the family income.

As she had planned, Janice posed as a social worker and Mrs Wilson seemed to see nothing strange in the arrangement.

'So you see, the baby's mother has had to have a serious operation and I don't need to tell you how pleased the department was to find someone like Sandra to look after him for a few weeks. It makes such a difference, too, when we know that he'll be in such a nice home as this.'

Janice could see the woman preening herself. 'Stupid old cow,' she said to herself, nevertheless managing to put on what she fondly hoped was a 'lady bountiful' smile. 'Well good-bye Mrs Wilson, thank you for the cup of tea.' As she climbed into her car, she managed to get Sandra to one side for a moment. 'I'll keep in touch with you by phone, O.K.?

Now promise me, not a word about whose baby he really is; if it gets out, there'll be hell to pay. Here's the first instalment of the money; I'll be sending you a similar amount each week.'

# 3

The burly man behind the desk read the reports in the buff folder through twice and then leaned back in his chair and closed his eyes. He sat there unmoving for several minutes and then reached for the phone.

'Come in,' he called out five minutes later in answer to the knock on the door. 'Ah, good morning Cathy, have a seat.' He pushed the folder across the desk. 'I'd like you to take this case on if it's at all possible; I have an instinct that it's going to prove extremely tricky and unfortunately I've got to take charge of that wretched corruption enquiry in the North in a couple of day's time. Have you got anything else on?'

'Well, I was due to go to that liaison meeting in Brussels, but if you don't mind if I miss that . . . '

Commander Kershaw gave a half smile. 'I think you know my views on those get togethers.'

'What's the case about sir?'

'There's not a great deal of information so far, but a ten month old baby called Mark Livingstone was taken from his pram in Hyde Park yesterday afternoon. It's not the usual run of things by any means; in the first place it was planned extremely carefully, an identical pram containing a pile of newspapers covered by a rug being substituted for the one with the sleeping baby in it while the nanny was distracted and secondly, the baby in question is the grandson of a High Court Judge.'

The slim young woman raised her eyebrows. 'Have the kidnappers communicated with the parents yet?'

'No.'

'Right you are then sir, I'll study the folder straight away.'

'You needn't worry about the two prams; there were no useful prints on either of them and I've already put Sergeant Playfair on to tracing the shop where the substitute one was bought — it was brand new and it shouldn't take him long.' Cathy Weston picked up the folder.

'One tip before you go; I had Judge Craythorne on the phone last night and I think it would pay you to see him first. Oh and Cathy.' The girl paused at the door. 'Sorry about Brussels.'

She gave him a smile. 'That's all right sir; there'll be other occasions.'

Kershaw watched her go, thinking that there were not all that many people who would have accepted his order without at least making some protest. Cathy Weston had been making regular visits to Brussels during the preceding six months and he happened to know that she had a boy-friend working in one of the EEC departments there. She had come a long way since she had started to work in his department and he had the highest opinion of her — he only hoped that this would be shared by Craythorne; by all accounts the Judge could be a crusty old devil.

★　★　★

Mr Justice Craythorne did not really approve of female police officers, any more than he approved of female barristers, let alone female judges, but he had to admit that there was something deeply reassuring about the calm young woman who faced him across the desk.

'I wanted to have a word with you before my son-in-law arrives Inspector,' he said. 'I think you'll see why in a moment. As you may imagine, ever since I heard the news I've hardly done anything else but think why this has happened. I suppose it could have been the impulsive action of some disturbed young woman, or even someone after ransom money, but what really worries me is that it may be a criminal psychopath out to get his own back on me.'

'Yes, I appreciate that. The switching of the prams, of course, makes it quite certain that it was premeditated, which in itself pretty well rules out your first suggestion.'

'That's true. I was trying a case like that a year or so ago and it's been my experience that such young women have either lost a baby recently or have had one adopted and do it on the spur of the moment and as you say, it could hardly be that.'

'What about the financial aspects? What does your son-in-law do?'

'He's a solicitor, but he doesn't touch criminal stuff; his practice is mainly conveyancing. He's comfortably off all right, but no more than that and the same could be said of me.'

'And your daughter?'

Craythorne fiddled with his pipe for a good minute before replying. 'You will appreciate that it's not easy for me to discuss distressing family matters with a stranger, but if you are going to help us . . . ' He cleared his throat and took a deep breath. 'My wife Dorothy was one of those people who are always either up in the clouds or in the depths of despair. I admit that our GP warned me that a child might be disastrous for her, but we both wanted one desperately and so we went ahead. He was right. After Mary was born, Dorothy went into one of those dreadful depressions that fail to respond to any form of treatment; she went into a mental hospital a month after Mary was born and was never able to come home. The doctors tried psychotherapy, chemo-therapy, sleep therapy, electro-convulsive therapy and indeed any therapy you care to mention, but nothing worked. Finally after five years, in despair I agreed to a leucotomy. I'm not blaming the psychia-trist or the surgeon, but that was no good either. When she finally died of pneumo-nia in the 1958 'flu epidemic, it was a blessed relief. Perhaps I did wrong, but when Mary was old enough to ask questions, Dorothy had made no progress for so long that I told her that her mother had died in childbirth. To this day, she and her husband believe it.

'You can imagine with what anxiety I watched Mary grow up. Should I have warned John about what had happened to her mother? Should I have warned them both about what might happen if Mary had a baby? It was true that Mary also had her ups and downs, but nothing really bad and they were so happy together. And so I kept putting off the decision and much as I wanted a grandchild, I felt a kind of relief when John told me that they had been trying for five years without success. It's ironic, isn't it, that she should have become pregnant within a few weeks of our conversation. I need hardly tell you what happened.' The judge sighed deeply. 'During the whole of her pregnancy Mary seemed radiant, the delivery was easy and the baby was a fine healthy boy, but within two weeks of the confinement my worst fears were realized. Mary was allowed to leave the mental hospital six weeks ago and she was just beginning to take an interest in Mark for the first time. I am not exaggerating when I say that this will kill her.'

'How has your son-in-law taken it?'

'You'll be meeting him in a minute or two and will no doubt be wanting to make your own judgement. He has rather a quick temper and you must remember what a tough time he has been through in the last nine months, but he has been a tower of strength and he certainly won't fold up under the strain of all this extra worry, but . . . Ah, that will be him now.'

Cathy was just about to tell him that he could trust her to respect his confidence, but the look that they exchanged as he got up to open the door put it more clearly than words would have been able to achieve.

John Livingstone was one of the largest young men that Cathy had ever seen, with a shock of unruly fair hair and piercing blue eyes. If the judge's disapproval of having a woman in charge of the case was barely perceptible, his was only too glaringly obvious.

'We already have the routine enquiries under way,' Cathy said after they had been introduced, 'and it seems to me that our most immediate concern must be with your wife.'

'If you think that she's in a fit state to answer a lot of questions, then you've got another think coming.'

'I was just going to suggest that it would probably be best if for the time being she knew nothing about it at all.'

'And how do you suppose we're going to achieve that?'

His voice and manner were barely civil

and Craythorne noted with approval that the young woman appeared to be quite unruffled.

'Perhaps she could go to stay with relatives. Your father-in-law was telling me that she hasn't been able to see very much of Mark and I was wondering if you would be able to get the suggestion across without letting her know that anything was wrong.'

'I'm sure that William and Elaine would be only too glad to help; you remember that they offered only the other day.'

Livingstone looked across at the judge and nodded curtly. 'All right, supposing that's a possibility, what then?'

'It seems to me that there are just two courses of action,' said Cathy, 'either we can wait until the kidnappers contact you, or we can put out Mark's picture on TV and in the newspapers and hope that we get a lead in that way.'

'What's your view Sir Arthur?'

'I'd be a bit wary about a lot of publicity in the media at this stage, it can make negotiations very difficult, you know.'

'Do you agree Inspector?'

'Yes I do. I don't think it would take a good reporter long to find out that your wife had been ill or where she was staying, which would immediately defeat our aim in keeping her out of it. Incidentally, do I look anything like her?'

'You're roughly the same build and colouring, but that's as far as it goes. Why do you ask?'

'Just that I was going to suggest that I come to stay in your house, if you have a spare room, that is. I would have thought that the most likely reason for Mark's kidnapping is that someone is trying to revenge themselves on Sir Arthur and if that is the case and they discover that your wife is ill and away from home, they might well make it their business to involve her directly. If I'm there to deal with anything that crops up, it might give us a useful lead.'

Livingstone's expression softened a fraction. 'You could have Miss Roberton's room; she's been so upset that I thought it best if I sent her off to stay with her sister.'

'Thank you, that sounds fine. With your permission, we'll put a tap on your phone and then I think we're as prepared as we can be.' Cathy consulted her notes. 'I see that you have a living-in house-keeper and her husband as well as Miss Robertson. Are you quite happy about them?'

'I can speak for the Trapnells,' replied the judge. 'They were with my brother for twenty years before he died and they are absolutely reliable. What about the nanny, John?'

'I took up her references, which were impeccable and I always had complete confidence in her.'

'Good,' said Cathy. 'When do you think you'll be able to make arrangements for your wife?'

'I'll have to confirm it of course, but I might be able to take her over to my sister-in-law this afternoon.'

'In that case, do you think I might meet you there and come back with you?'

'I suppose you're thinking that these people might be watching the house already.'

'That's right and it'll solve the problem of getting me inside the house without arousing suspicion.'

Livingstone didn't seem to Cathy to give the suggestion exactly a rapturous approval, but at least she felt she had won the old judge over; it was not that he said anything, but as she left, he gave her hand a firm squeeze and there was no doubt in her mind that his smile was both genuine and warm.

★ ★ ★

Cathy spent the afternoon interviewing Miss Robertson in Streatham, but the old Scotswoman was unable to help very much and it was obvious that she had been quite shattered by the experience. She was still too upset to be able to think clearly and her description of the girl who had twisted her ankle was quite useless — when it came to detail, she couldn't even remember the colour of her hair. After a few minutes, when it was obvious that she wasn't going to get anywhere with that, she turned to the subject of the

Livingstones, but apart from saying how kind they were, the old nanny was quite unable to elaborate. She kept crying quietly to herself and after a short time, Cathy decided that it would be kinder to leave her in peace. One thing was very clear and that was that her distress was quite genuine.

When she arrived at the house in Chelsea with John Livingstone, Cathy introduced herself to Mrs Trapnell and had a late cup of tea with her in the basement. The woman had obviously taken her instructions not to talk about the whole affair very much to heart and hardly said a word, but Cathy had the strong impression that that wouldn't last once she had been there a few days.

The rest of that evening had a totally unreal quality to it, she had supper with John Livingstone, they listened to some records and made polite and stilted conversation. He was perfectly civil to her, but there was an uncomfortable constraint between them and once or twice she caught him looking at her in a way that made her wonder about the wisdom of her decision to stay under the same roof as him.

Kershaw, and for that matter her own family, thought that she had a boy-friend in Brussels, but the truth of the matter was that she had made him up to stop everyone from teasing her. Not for the first time, she wondered if she was ever going to be able to overcome her fears of men. Other girls didn't seem to have her problems, but then other girls hadn't been conditioned by their mother's constant warnings and cautions. If only she had been through the normal adolescent petting phase, perhaps she wouldn't have had her present hangups and could have behaved more naturally with the men who took her out, whom she either seemed to bore to distraction or who obviously had one aim and one aim only. Was it so strange that she wanted to wait until after she got married? Her real fear, though, was that no one might ask her and if they did, it might be no better then. Another of her troubles was that she had very little understanding of the way men thought;

she realized that most probably a lot of the things they said to her were all part of the same game that other girls seemed to enjoy — if only she had been able to take herself less seriously!

As she watched Livingstone, she realized that if she had had any sensitivity at all, she would have understood what a strain having her under the same roof would put on him, when his wife had obviously shown no interest in him at all since the baby had been born. She did her best to be friendly, but at the same time kept her distance and excused herself as early as she possibly could.

'Have you everything you need up there?'

'Yes thank you. The telephone people have put an extension in my room and if it goes in the night, I'll let you answer it and then listen in myself. It'll all be recorded, but obviously we'll have to play it by ear. Cheer up,' she said, feeling she couldn't leave him looking so utterly woebegone, 'I'm sure we'll get your little boy back.'

He stared at her with his very blue eyes. 'I wish I was able to share your optimism.'

★　★　★

The call came about an hour after Cathy had fallen into an uneasy sleep. She switched on the light, saw that it was a few minutes after three a.m. and lifted the receiver after the bell had stopped ringing.

'John Livingstone here.'

'Mr Livingstone,' the voice had an odd muffled quality to it, 'I wish to speak to your wife.'

'She's not been well, she's . . . '

'If you want to see your child again, you'll put her on the line at once.'

'Hello,' said Cathy after a short interval.

'Beginning to sweat a little, are you?' The man gave a chuckle.

'What do you want? What have you done with my baby?'

'Listen carefully; if you wish to get him back, this is what you have to do.' The instructions were given briefly and concisely. 'Is that quite clear?'

'Yes.'

'Repeat it all back to me.'

Her reply was received in complete silence. 'Are you still there? When are you going to return Mark to me?' For a few seconds all she could hear was the sound of heavy breathing. 'Please tell me.'

'You'll hear from me again when we have received the money. If you inform the police about this or make any attempt to set up a trap, I tell you, you'll regret it.'

'Where will . . . ' Her question was cut off by a loud click, followed by the dialling tone.

Cathy put on her dressing gown and went down to Livingstone's bedroom. He was sitting on the edge of the bed with his head in his hands and looked up as she came in.

'Why do you suppose they want Mary to take the ransom money?'

'It all fits in with the idea that they are trying to get at Sir Arthur through your wife and baby. Can you raise the £20,000?'

'With my father-in-law's help I could,' he said slowly. 'Are you suggesting that I should just pay up.'

'Let's look at it this way; we could hand

over the money and hope that that's all they're after; we could take the money to the station as they suggest and try to identify and follow the people who collect it, or we could use paper instead of money and still go after them.'

'The money's of no importance compared with Mark's safety; the question is whether or not we can trust them to keep their side of the bargain.'

'I for one don't think we can. We've got two days to set something up at the station and I reckon we should be able to get a lead without any risk of them finding out. I wouldn't want to press you though, and if you would like me to hand over the money in exactly the way they suggest, you've only got to say.'

'I'd like to talk it over with Sir Arthur first.'

'Of course. Perhaps you'd give me a ring here later this morning as soon as you've seen him.'

'All right.'

Cathy would dearly have liked to offer him some words of comfort, but she had seen that look of his again and drew her dressing-gown more tightly across her chest.

'Good night.'

Livingstone didn't reply and when she glanced back from the door-way, his face was once more buried in his hands.

★ ★ ★

Cathy went to see Commander Kershaw late that morning as soon as Livingstone had telephoned.

'How's it going?' he asked.

'You've heard the tape recording sir?' Kershaw nodded. 'Well, I've got Livingstone's permission to have our men at Waterloo, but understandably he doesn't want any risk of the kidnappers finding out, in case they retaliate.'

'That's a bit of a tall order, I must say. What exactly had you in mind?'

'I thought I'd see the electronics people straight away; I'm sure they will be able to put a transmitter into the hold-all I use to take the money to the station and I'll have to see if they can give me anything small enough to stick on to a second carrier if they tell me to transfer it. Then, if we have a car at both ends of the access road and cover all the pedestrian exits with men equipped with radios, we should be able to follow the person who picks up the money without too much difficulty.'

'Hmm . . . I don't like it much, but I suppose it's the best we can do.' He saw her look of disappointment. 'I wasn't meaning to criticize your plan, but I've seen this sort of thing go wrong before. How's Livingstone taking it?'

'The atmosphere's not exactly comfortable and I have the strong feeling that he'll be only too ready to blame us if anything goes wrong. I did warn him, of course, that unless we run a substantial risk of making our presence known, we might not get anywhere, but . . . '

'Not to worry, the policeman's lot and all that. Now look, I have to leave tomorrow; Commander Osborne will be in over-all charge if you run into any major difficulties, but in addition to that, you'll certainly need some help on the ground.' He looked down at the list in front of him. 'How about Gould?'

Cathy's hesitation was only momentary and her expression hardly altered, but Kershaw's sharp eyes picked it up.

'Yes, he'd be fine.'

He picked up the phone and let out an almost inaudible sigh as he waited for the detective to be found. He had thought that Cathy had managed to solve her personal difficulties after the Gibson case, but it looked as if he had been wrong; he had enough on his plate without having to act as unpaid nurse-maid as well. As soon as he had had the thought, he regretted it; the young policewoman had had a very bad time during that investigation and perhaps it wasn't so surprising that she was still feeling insecure with members of the opposite sex.

★ ★ ★

Jim Gould was having a cup of coffee in the canteen when he was called to the telephone.

'What's up?' his friend asked when he got back.

'Just old man Kershaw — he wants me to do a job with Cathy Weston.'

'I know one job you won't be doing with her mate.'

'What makes you so sure about that?'

'I tell you, she'd be better off in a convent than in a place like this.'

'You're just jealous, that's your trouble Alan; it's being shut up with those dusty records all day — no wonder you get all these unhealthy thoughts.'

'Believe me mate, I know what I'm talking about.'

'So she turned you down, did she old son? She's got more taste than I suspected.'

The other man hit him on the head with a rolled up newspaper. 'I tell you what, I bet you a fiver you can't make it with her.'

'Don't be so daft.'

'There you are. The trouble with you Jim is that you've got no class, no class at all. I always did think that you were just a typists' pool man.'

Gould was about to say that there was nothing wrong with the girls in the typing pool, but decided to leave before he lost his temper — somehow Thurston always managed to needle him. It didn't make him feel any better when he remembered the last time he had seen Cathy Weston and it was a surprise to him that she had agreed to work on the same case.

Only two weeks earlier, he had been with a group of friends in one of the offices and he had been retelling a story that he had heard about her from one of the men who had been to Brussels with her. He had mistaken their sudden silence for anticipation of the climax of the story.

'And then our prim Miss Weston asked: 'have you had a check-up recently?' 'No,' replied this Belgian bird, 'only a Pole actually.' '

Instead of the expected howl of laughter, the end of the story had been greeted with a stony silence. He had turned round slowly to see Cathy Weston standing in the open door-way. She had looked at him coldly and then walked off without a word. He hadn't seen her since.

If she was embarrassed by having to work with him, she managed not to show it and he forced himself to concentrate on what she was saying, trying to forget his conversation with the lecherous Alan Thurston.

'What do you think?' she said finally.

'I've never been on a kidnap case before, but from what I've read, they're nothing but woe. I think your plan's a very good one.' He took another look at the lay-out of Waterloo Station which had been drawn out in a large scale. 'I'll have to go and have a look round to see if we can mount a TV camera anywhere, although I must say that it doesn't look as if it would be all that easy or necessarily very rewarding.'

'Right. Perhaps, though, you'd come with me to see the electronics bloke first?'

Mr Cuthbert — everyone, even the Commissioner called him that — was small and almost completely bald. He was obviously an enthusiast and demonstrated all his apparatus with loving care. Cathy was amazed to see how tiny some of the transmitters were and the ingenious ways in which they were hidden in all sorts of objects.

Mr Cuthbert looked at the Living-stones' hold-all with great care.

'It all depends, of course, on how big a range you require on the one hand and how anxious you are for it to be undetected on the other. If I put a really small one in, it would be very difficult to find, but you wouldn't get a range of more than thirty feet.'

Gould frowned. 'That wouldn't be anything like far enough for us — a hundred yards is what we need; we might have to keep track of it in a car.'

'I see, in that case we'll have to use the handle. One of the problems is the question of batteries and an aerial; it would be perfectly possible to hide it all, but I'm afraid it would be very easy to detect if anyone looked properly.'

'But surely any device like this that transmits a signal can be picked up by an appropriate receiver.'

'Yes, that's perfectly true, but if this gang is as sophisticated as that, you'd have no hope at all of it remaining undetected. You'll just have to decide whether the risk is acceptable or not.'

'Can you put a switch on it so that I can turn it off if I have to transfer the money to another container?'

'Yes, that would be quite simple.'

'And then I'd want something small that I could stick or pin to any alternative bag they produce.'

'Anything else?'

'One last thing; I will need to be in constant contact with Inspector Gould. What have you got in the way of two-way radios Mr Cuthbert?'

'Let's see now, perhaps something round the neck would be best — I have a selection here.'

Cathy looked through the objects set out on the table and finally picked up a silver locket; she turned it round and opened the front panel where she found a faded photograph.

'What a beautiful piece,' she said, inspecting the hall-mark. Looking up, she saw the little man's smile. 'You can't mean it.'

'I'm afraid it's not so good as it looks; the microphone and loud-speaker are the only things in it. The batteries and the rest of the apparatus have to be carried elsewhere — we usually use something like a belt or a specially padded bra. For the time being, just strap this round your waist and I'll connect it up to the chain. Right, now press the catch on the bottom.'

Cuthbert signalled to the man behind the glass panel at the end of the room and faintly, but quite distinctly, Cathy heard a voice coming from the locket.

'Can you hear me? Turn the knob at the base if you want greater volume.'

'It's perfect. What a wonderful piece of work.'

Cuthbert beamed with pleasure. 'If you want to transmit, all you have to do is press the button on the side there. You can keep it as a souvenir when you've finished with it, if you like.'

Cathy took it off and held it in her hand. 'May I really? It must be quite valuable.'

'It's a fake, I'm afraid, but I'm glad you chose it, I was rather pleased with it myself. Now, perhaps you'd go into the cubicle there and let me have the bra you're wearing. There'll be no problem about it fitting comfortably and we can get to work on it straight away.'

Gould hastily wiped the grin off his face, but she had seen it and hesitated fractionally before replying. 'All right.'

'I'll have it and the hold-all sent round to you this evening.'

Gould took Cathy back to the house in Chelsea by car. It was only too obvious that she hadn't selected her blouse to be worn without anything underneath, but he found the effect quite delightful and had considerable difficulty in restraining himself from checking up to see just how delightful it was every few minutes.

'Good luck tomorrow,' he said as she got out of the car, 'I won't let you down.'

As she bent down to reply, his eyes were drawn irresistibly towards the top button of her blouse and she coloured slightly.

'I know you won't.'

Gould nodded to the constable on duty outside and drove off, thinking that one day he might manage to avoid giving her the impression that he was an over-sexed adolescent with nothing else on his mind.

★  ★  ★

Cathy found the afternoon dragging interminably. Jim Gould was busy making arrangements at the station and she passed the time trying to classify the various people whom Judge Craythorne had sentenced in the preceding few years. Within minutes, she knew that it wasn't going to get her anywhere; in one vice trial alone, there had been fifteen defendants and God alone knew how many other shadowy figures behind the scenes. However, she persevered and by the late afternoon had them in some sort of order.

The more Cathy saw of Livingstone, the more difficult did she find it to behave naturally with him; she frankly disliked the man, whom she thought a bully and to make matters worse, she was more then a little scared of him, so much so that when he came close to her, she found it almost impossible not to shrink away.

'I do wish you'd stop staring at me,' he said, after a particularly long silence at the supper table.

'I'm sorry — it's just that I'm a bit nervous about tomorrow.'

'That's hardly something that fills me with confidence, I must say,' he replied acidly.

After that, she gave up trying to make conversation and went up to her room as soon as she decently could.

★ ★ ★

The following morning, Cathy set out for Waterloo Station in the Livingstones' car. She had felt quite self-conscious about putting on the bra containing the electrical equipment as although it had been most skilfully done and was quite comfortable, it did make her look distinctly pneumatic.

As instructed, she parked in the 'limited waiting' area outside the station and a few minutes before eleven o'clock, walked through the tall arch into the fore-court, the hold-all in her hand. Cathy seldom travelled by train and in any case had not been to Waterloo for years, so was unfamiliar with the lay-out;

she had been told to go to the phone booth nearest to platform 17 and when she arrived in front of the row of ten of them, was surprised to find that they were open fronted, being separated from their neighbours only by half partitions.

She had switched on her receiver when she entered the station, but even though she was expecting it, practically jumped out of her skin when the voice came up from the locket.

'We have you in sight; one of our men is close to you as well. Good luck.'

All the booths were occupied and in addition, several people were waiting their turn. Cathy stood a few feet from the one at the end of the row and while she waited impatiently for the girl to finish her seemingly interminable conversation, she looked casually around. No one seemed to be paying her the slightest attention. At last the booth became vacant and according to her instructions, she began to leaf through the directory, at the same time looking to see if a message had been left anywhere.

She pressed the button on the locket

and hid her mouth with her hand. 'I haven't found anything so far. Over.'

'Hang on there. We have been watching that booth for twenty-four hours and nobody suspicious has been anywhere near it. They will probably ring you. Keep you instrument set to transmit. Over.'

'Message understood.'

Cathy was just beginning to feel that she had been brought on a fool's errand, when the bell began to ring. She snatched up the receiver, moving the locket so that it was as close to the ear-piece as possible.

'You are being observed carefully.' The voice was the same one she had heard before. 'Do precisely what you are told. To your left, in front of the entrance to platform twelve, is a booth with a sliding door where people can make their own recordings; it will be empty — there is an 'out of order' notice on the handle. Remove the notice, go inside, shutting the door tightly behind you, transfer the money to the brief-case you'll find on the floor and then wait there for precisely five minutes. At the end of that time, leave the brief-case on the floor, leaning against the wall opposite the door. When you depart, leave the door fully open and walk back to your car with the empty hold-all without looking back. Now, repeat the instructions back to me.'

Immediately she had done so, the caller rang off and she put the microphone to her lips. 'Did you hear all that, over?'

'Yes. Proceed as directed; we will be covering you.'

Cathy found the miniature recording studio without difficulty. She removed the notice stuck to the handle with a piece of sellotape, stepped inside and pulled the door behind her. The black brief-case made out of cheap plastic material was resting on the floor. The booth was about four feet long by three wide and was lined by sound proofing material, perforated by small holes; she was soon made aware that it was quite effective — not only was the noise from the station largely cut off, but she was unable to get any response from the two-way radio.

She couldn't help wondering if the kidnappers had devised some means of getting the brief-case out other than through the door and she looked around carefully, but it was immediately obvious that this would be an impossibility. In the wall immediately in front of her were two microphones set into the panelling and each was covered with wire mesh, a red light and the instructions being immediately above them. The lettering was faded and chipped, but she was able to make it out without difficulty.

FOR BEST RESULTS KEEP SLIDING
DOOR CLOSED
STAND BACK AND SPEAK CLEARLY
SPEAK WHEN RED
LIGHT IS ON

Just above face level, there was a rectangle of reinforced glass and through it, she could see the recording apparatus. In the same wall were set the slot for inserting the money, a green light, the shute for rejected coins and a slit for collecting the recording. The only other item of interest was the inevitable collection of graffiti on the wood-work.

In the five minutes available, Cathy had

ample time in which to transfer the money, insert the tiny transmitter through a hole in the stitching and switch off the device in her own hold-all. When the time was up, she positioned the brief-case against the wall and opened the door. There was quite a crowd outside — a train had just arrived at the platform opposite — and she did not dare to use her transmitter in case one of the kidnappers was within earshot. Without hesitating or looking back, she walked across the road that split the fore-court into two halves and made for the car. She had only gone about fifty yards, when she heard a shout behind her.

'Hey! I say!'

She turned round and saw a young man, holding his bowler hat in one hand and clutching the brief-case in the other, running towards her. She just had time to think that he had wrecked the whole operation, when she realized that he had not seen the post office van which was leaving the station. She opened her mouth to shout a warning, but she was too late; there was a squeal of brakes, the van swerved violently to one side and the man was sent sprawling on to the ground, the brief-case skidding over the tarmac and under a trolley. By the time Cathy got to him, the young man was beginning to pick himself up and with every minute, more and more people were beginning to gather round.

'Are you all right?' Cathy asked anxiously.

'Yes thanks, no great harm done. Stupid of me, I never saw the van until it was too late.'

An enormously fat woman wearing a voluminous plastic mac came waddling up with the brief-case, pushed it into Cathy's hand, acknowledged her thanks with a nod and walked away again with a surprising turn of speed, breathing heavily. Another ten minutes went by before all the excitement had settled; the driver of the van had to be calmed down, someone insisted on buying the young man a cup of tea and his umbrella and raincoat had to be rescued from in front of the recording booth.

Eventually, Cathy managed to extricate

herself from the crowd and walked back to the car. When she got behind the wheel, she opened the brief-case to check the money and saw something which took the colour from her cheeks; held together with elastic bands were neat packets of blank paper.

★   ★   ★

Janice had seen the whole thing from a nearby magazine and newspaper stall, but even though she was watching carefully and knew roughly how they were going to do it, she missed seeing the actual switch. Grey had explained the idea to her that day in the club.

'I am proposing to work on the assumption that the police will be watching,' he had said. 'That means that we will have to employ someone who, if caught, can be relied on not to talk.' He had smiled grimly. 'Adrian Bruce will do very well; he was at school with me and is a most respectable civil servant and I have no doubt that he will do exactly what he is told. He is a particularly apt choice, if

I may say so; he always did have a talent for amateur dramatics.' He had then turned his snake-like eyes in her direction. 'One word of advice to you; you are paying and paying heavily for the privilege of being there when that woman arrives with the money, but if by your presence you alert the police and if any of my men are caught as the result of your stupidity . . . '

He hadn't needed to say anything further. Janice felt the hairs on the back of her neck rise as he continued to fix her with his icy stare.

'I know what I'm doing; I'm not a complete beginner, you know.'

He had looked pointedly at her hands which still had not fully recovered from her time in prison.

'I can see that.'

Janice's first surprise came when she saw Mary Livingstone come out of the recording booth. The tall, slim girl with the long black hair was much younger than she had expected and also much calmer looking, nothing like the distraught, agitated woman of her imagination. It was acutely disappointing in one way, but most certainly not in another; the thin veneer of control would soon crack and by the time she had finished, she'd have that cool-looking bitch grovelling at her feet.

A few moments after Mary Livingstone started to walk away from the booth, Janice saw a rather vacuous-looking young man in a pin-stripe suit and wearing a bowler hat, approach. She had to admit that he put on an extremely convincing show. He appeared to catch sight of the brief-case and made a gesture towards Mary Livingstone's back with his umbrella, at the same time giving her a shout.

When she failed to look round, he dived into the booth, tripping over the small step and falling to his knees. After he had backed out again and started towards the retreating woman, waving the briefcase in the air, Janice was so convinced that he had made the switch already, that she was still watching the booth when she heard the screech of brakes and saw the crowd collecting near the post office van.

By the time it was all over, however, she was by no means convinced that Bruce hadn't lost his nerve; not only had she seen that the next person to go into the booth was a small boy, who came out again almost at once empty handed, but she had also watched Mary Livingstone walk back to her car with the brief-case firmly in her hand. Indeed, Janice was only finally convinced when she collected the money from the club later that afternoon.

'That went very smoothly,' she said when she was shown into Grey's office. 'It's a pleasure to do business with you.'

'It's as well for you that it did,' he replied coldly, tapping the desk gently with an ornate paper knife. Does the name of Mr Justice Craythorne ring any bells with you?'

All the colour left Janice's cheeks. 'I don't know what you mean.'

'Let me spell it out for you then. If my men hadn't been seriously at fault in failing to check on this Mrs Livingstone of yours in time and, what's more, tried to cover it up, I might have vented my spleen on you rather than them. I don't like people who aren't entirely honest with me, but I'll overlook it this once. As it is, though, we're going to have to set up the second part of the exercise with even greater care and it's going to cost you a great deal more, unless of course you want to forget about the whole thing.'

Janice was furious. She pointed out that they already had an agreement, that it had been his fault for employing half-wits; she even suggested that he was getting cold feet. She slowly dried up, though, when to her astonishment, he got up and poured her a drink.

'I find myself developing a grudging admiration for your courage — some would call it foolhardiness — but don't press your luck too hard. I am still prepared to mount the rest of the operation because it intrigues me and because I personally have no great love for your precious judge. You can see Mulligan outside; he has had the money changed for you in case it was marked and you will find that my revised fee has been deducted. He will also be able to give you details of the new plan.'

Janice opened her mouth to speak again, but then decided to bide her time; one day her opportunity would come and then . . .

'It might also interest you to know,' he said when she was half way to the door, 'that Mrs Livingstone will be receiving her present tomorrow morning.'

# 4

Cathy had thought it safest to drive straight back to Chelsea in the Livingstones' car and had an agonizing wait until Gould rang up. He was fairly non-committal over the phone, but when she met him at the Yard after lunch, she saw at once how excited he was.

'The actual switch was done by that woman in the plastic mac.'

'The one who brought the brief-case back to me?'

'That's right.'

'How did you discover that?'

'Stephens was covering her while I looked after the man in the bowler hat. After she gave you the brief-case, she sat down on a bench only a few feet away and started to collect a great pile of hand luggage together. All this time, of course, you were still in the vicinity and he thought that the strong signal he was still receiving was coming from the one she gave back to you. Nevertheless, he continued to watch her; after a few minutes, she got up and went towards the ladies and as you can imagine, he assumed she was in the clear when he lost the signal after she had gone about thirty yards. He waited for her to come out, but didn't see her and was still hanging about in front of the ladies when we found the empty brief-case, which was hidden under the bench where she had been sitting and which was still transmitting merrily. She must have moved the money under cover of that plastic mac, which we found, together with the hat she had been wearing, in one of the cubicles in the cloakroom.'

'And so I suppose she got clean away with the money?'

'Yes she did.'

Cathy thought for a moment or two. 'But if you're right about that, the man with the bowler hat must have been involved as well.'

'Right in one. I followed him to his office and for good measure nicked his wallet, which has since been returned to him with the compliments of British Rail.'

'Who is he?'

'Bloke by the name of Bruce; he works in the Foreign Office and his father's a big-wig in the Treasury.'

'Seems an unlikely candidate for a job like that, I must say.'

'Not if someone's putting the black on him.'

'Did he have a good reason for being at Waterloo at that particular time?'

'Yes. He was late into work because of an emergency dental appointment. He stayed the previous night with his parents in Esher and that's also where the dentist works and explains his presence at Waterloo. I had a slice of luck with the dentist; one of the blokes on the Force in Esher happens to know him and he found out that one of Bruce's fillings had cracked.'

'Did he think it had happened spontaneously, or had someone interfered with it?'

'I asked about that, but evidently he wasn't prepared to say.'

'When was the appointment made?'

'A couple of days ago.'

'If you're right about this chap Bruce, Jim — and I can't see any other possible explanation — it all seems to have been planned remarkably carefully.'

'Yes, but not carefully enough. As I said, they must have some sort of hold over him and we've got to find out what and quickly.'

'That sounds a bit of a tall order. Did you find anything useful in his wallet?'

Gould handed over a couple of photographs. 'Not much really, just these two membership cards.'

'They don't mean anything to me I'm afraid.'

'One's for a gambling club and the others for a rather sleazy dining establishment where they go in for topless waitresses.'

'What do you reckon should be our next move?'

'I'll see if the Whitehall security people know anything about Bruce — they should be able to think of a way of putting the screws on him if anyone can.'

'You've done wonders already Jim, I

only hope that our friend Livingstone thinks so too.'

'Are you sure you're all right alone there with him?'

'The Trapnells are only a couple of floors down in the basement.'

'Well, if I were you, I'd lock your bedroom door; from what you've told me, he sounds a right bastard.'

Cathy coloured slightly. 'I think I can handle him.'

★   ★   ★

Livingstone was once again barely civil when he got back from his office; he poured himself a large whisky without offering her anything and paced up and down as she told him what had happened.

'What it really amounts to is that they've got the £20,000, Mark's not been returned and you've achieved sweet Fanny Adams.'

'That's quite unfair and you know it. We've protected your wife and we've managed to get a good lead on one of their men without letting on that we've done it. Look Mr Livingstone, why don't we . . . '

'Don't you look me, young woman. I'll tell you one thing, if it wasn't for the fact that Craythorne supplied most of that money and insisted that I went along with this charade, you'd have been out of here long since.'

Livingstone swallowed the rest of the whisky in one gulp, ran down the stairs and went out into the street. He walked without knowing or caring where his legs were carrying him and an hour and a half later, when the blister on his heel could be ignored no longer, pushed his way roughly through the door of a pub. It was situated on the corner of a street on the end of a long row of mean looking houses, which had obviously been scheduled for destruction; most of their windows had long since been broken and a number of the doors had been boarded up.

The rough looking man behind the bar stopped polishing the glass he was holding and looked up warily; to say that he was unused to seeing men in dark suits coming into the pub would have been a major understatement.

'Yes . . . sir.' The pause was just long enough to be insulting.

'Whisky. And you can cut out the funny stuff, I'm not in the mood.'

The man opened his mouth to reply, but took another look at the enormous width of the shoulders only three feet from him and rapidly changed his mind.

Livingstone was nearing the end of his fourth double when he became aware of the woman who had been sitting for some time on the stool next to him. He crinkled his nose in disgust as he took in her clumsily applied make-up, the greasy hair and the short leather skirt. He needed a woman, by God he did, but had not sunk as low as that yet. He and Mary had been so happy in that way. He felt his eyes beginning to prick and angrily got off the stool and made his way unsteadily out of the door.

It was in the taxi on his way home that it slowly dawned on him that the solution to his problem was lying neatly tucked up in the bed in the spare room upstairs in his house. The girl was young and attractive and the fact that she was obviously scared of him, added enormously to his excitement. She would no doubt put up some resistance for form's sake, but he managed to convince himself that some of the looks she had given him suggested that she wanted it as much as he did.

'Oh it's you Mr Livingstone. Everything all right then sir?'

'Yes thank you constable. All quiet here?'

'Nothing to report at all.'

'Fine. 'Night.'

He struggled with the key for several minutes before realizing that it was the one from the office.

'Wrong one,' he said, giving the policeman a conspiratorial wink.

Livingstone plunged his face into a basinful of cold water, cleaned his teeth and then slowly went up the stairs. He hesitated for a moment outside her room, but then he remembered what she had looked like when she had come downstairs two nights earlier. He took a firm grip on the handle, turned it and pushed. His fury when he found that the door was immovable was so great that for a moment he was stunned into inactivity.

'My God!' he said to himself 'the bitch has locked herself in — and in my house!'

He rattled the handle and shook the door as hard as he could.

'Miss Weston!' he shouted. 'I want to speak to you.' There was a long silence and he pounded on the panelling. 'Please — let me in.'

'I'll see you tomorrow morning Mr Livingstone — it's too late now.'

He shouted, he threatened, he pleaded with her and finally put his shoulder to the door and hit it with a crash that reverberated around the landing.

'If you don't go away, I'll be forced to ring for help. You're upset and you've had too much to drink — go to bed.'

The voice was a little tremulous, but nonetheless had authority in it and he was just sober enough to understand that she meant what she said. He gave the door a savage kick and blundered down the stairs into his own room, where he lay on the bed, face down, pounding the pillow with his fist.

★   ★   ★

Livingstone did not appear for breakfast the following morning and Cathy was glancing through the morning paper when she heard the front doorbell. A short time later Mrs Trapnell appeared with a parcel, which was neatly done up in brown paper.

'It was recorded delivery and addressed to Mrs Livingstone, so I thought it best if I brought it up straight away.'

'Thank you Mrs Trapnell.'

It was at that moment that Livingstone appeared at the door in his dressing gown; he looked pale and drawn, hadn't shaved and his eyes were bloodshot.

'Come and have a cup of coffee.'

He sat down heavily and then waited until the housekeeper had left the room.

'About last night.' He paused for a long time. 'I'm deeply sorry — it won't happen again.'

Cathy realized just how much it must

have cost him to say even that much and decided to pass it off as lightly and as quickly as possible.

'That's quite all right — I understand.' She picked up the parcel. 'Was your wife expecting anything to be delivered?'

'She didn't say anything to me about it. Have you asked Mrs Trapnell?'

'Yes, and she hadn't heard anything about it either. With your permission, I'd like to take it round to our lab and get the experts to open it.'

'Do you have to go to all that trouble?'

'Yes, I think I should. It's only too easy to put an explosive device into a packet like this and I don't think we should run unnecessary risks.'

'Oh all right then.'

Cathy tried to be as encouraging as possible, but Livingstone remained morose and uncommunicative and it was a relief for her to get out of the house.

*   *   *

Ferguson, the man on duty in the forensic laboratory was an enthusiast and took a profound delight in his job. His eyes lit up when he saw Cathy; his other main hobby was needling his colleagues, particularly those who did not share his passionate interest in the macabre and he had heard that she was more susceptible than most. He had had coffee with Cuthbert that morning and this gave him inspiration.

'Got your talking bra on today then, my love?'

Cathy put down the parcel on the bench and fingered the locket round her neck. 'As a matter of fact I have and it's transmitting at this very moment to Commander Osborne's office — he wanted to hear about the parcel at the earliest possible opportunity. Did you want to speak to him or something?'

Ferguson went pale, but then saw the expression on her face. 'You rotten so and so, I've a good mind to . . . '

Cathy lifted up the parcel and pretended to throw it at him. The man flinched and passed his hand across his forehead.

'Don't do things like that, my dear; my heart won't stand it.'

'All right; let's call it quits shall we?'

The man stared at her for a moment and then smiled and inspected the box carefully. 'What's the story behind this?'

Cathy told him in detail. 'And so you see this Mrs Livingstone's been ill for a long time and it's most unlikely that she would have ordered anything by post and neither her husband nor the housekeeper know anything about it. I was afraid that it might contain an explosive.'

Ferguson lifted it up and put it in a pair of scales. 'Hmm — if that's the case, there's enough inside to blow up a whole house. Now, the next item on the agenda is to get it X-rayed.'

The film came out of the drier a few minutes later and the man put it up on the viewing box.

'What on earth is it?'

'Your friends are not nice people at all; it's a foot, a baby's foot.'

A smile flitted across Ferguson's face; he thought it would knock the stuffing out of her and he wasn't disappointed; all the colour went from her face and for a moment, he thought she was going to faint.

He tapped the film with a pointer. 'You can see the bones here, but it's not all that clear. Hang on a jiffy and I'll open the box and be able to give you a proper report.'

Cathy had to make a tremendous effort not to be physically sick when Ferguson brought the foot in on an enamel tray some fifteen minutes later.

'No distinguishing marks,' he said, turning it over with a pair of forceps, 'a child about a year old, the bone has been sawn through — that's about all I can tell you about it. Oh yes. It was packed in ice in a plastic bag, probably this morning, so it looks as if your post-man was bogus.'

Cathy thought hard for a few moments. 'Assuming that this is just a ghastly sick joke on their part, is there anywhere they might have got a baby's foot?'

'I suppose they could have bribed a post-mortem attendant at a hospital or a crematorium.'

'Can you think of any way of proving that the foot isn't Mark Livingstone's? I couldn't face having to ask either of his parents or the old nanny for that matter.'

'We might be able to do it through blood grouping, but to achieve that we would either have to know the boy's group, or that of both his parents. You do realize, of course, that even then the result is quite likely to prove inconclusive.'

'You mean that the group of the blood in the foot might be the same as Mark's just by coincidence?'

'Yes, either that or the same as one of his parents.'

'How likely is it?'

'Very — something like eighty per cent of the population is either O positive or A positive.' Ferguson saw the expression on her face and realized at once that she was emotionally involved with the case. Just like a woman, he thought, and smiled cynically at the young inspector. 'If you ask me, you'll just have to ask the mother along.'

Cathy had had enough. 'No one is asking you, Ferguson. Now let's have that blood group and make it snappy, will you? I haven't got all day.'

'My, my, we are touchy, aren't we?'

'How to win friends and influence people,' she said to herself, as the man left the room muttering to himself.

★　★　★

A couple of hours later, Cathy had lunch with Jim Gould in the canteen.

'How have you got on?' he asked when they were settled at a table in the corner.

'It turned out all right in the end, but I wouldn't want to go through the first part of the morning again in a hurry.' She told him what had happened in the forensic laboratory. 'I was jolly lucky to get hold of Mark Livingstone's blood group so easily and then they were able to prove that the foot wasn't his.'

'How did you get it?'

'I found out that Mark was born at St Gregory's Hospital and after that, it was quite easy. As Mrs Livingstone is Rhesus negative, they grouped the baby in case of difficulties and he turned out to be O positive; the blood in the foot was A positive.'

'But what a horrible thing for those kidnappers to have done.'

'Yes, there's undoubtedly a criminal psychopath on the loose; in a way I could have understood them doing something like that if the Livingstones had refused to pay the ransom, but . . . Think what it would have done to Mary Livingstone if she had opened the parcel herself.'

'What are you going to tell John Livingstone?'

'I see no point in bothering him with it; I'll make up something or other to explain the parcel. How about you? Did you get any lines on Bruce?'

'Well, you know how close these security blokes are, particularly if they think that one is treading on their cherished preserves, but I was lucky enough to be put on to a bloke called Harding, who couldn't have been more helpful. Bruce works in a fairly minor capacity in the FO, but his father's a big noise in the Treasury and they're most anxious that this should be handled with kid gloves.'

'Do you think that they might try to hush it up?'

'No, I don't think so. Indeed, although he didn't actually spell it out, Harding suggested that he might be able to put pressure on Bruce in ways that we couldn't.'

'It sounds all very cloak and dagger, I must say. What exactly had he in mind?'

'He suggested that I went with him tonight to that gambling club — you remember Bruce had the membership card in his wallet and evidently he goes there practically every evening. Harding's also a member and he's proposing 'to stir Bruce up a bit' as he put it. Why don't you come with us? You must be dying to get away from that bloke Livingstone.'

'But suppose Bruce recognizes me?'

'He won't, not if you're in your best bib and tucker. Go on, a night out will do you good.'

Cathy had in fact been dreading another evening alone with Livingstone and it might be fun — she had never been to a gambling club and the more she saw of Gould, the more she liked him.

'All right then.'

'Great. You never know, you might win a fortune.'

Gould watched her walk down the corridor and when she had disappeared suddenly saw Alan Thurston standing at the door with a grin on his face.

'Have you won that bet yet? You seemed to be having a very cosy chat there.'

'Do you know something Alan? She's a thoroughly nice person and that's something you'll never be.'

The man clicked his teeth together. 'Aye, aye, you've really got the hots for her haven't you?'

'You're asking for one up the snout, my friend.'

'And who's going to . . . '

'Ah Gould! Just the man I was looking for.' Commander Osborne took him by the arm. 'Come along to my office, will you? I'd like you to fill me on this case.'

Thurston watched them out of sight and fingered his jaw pensively.

115

# 5

Right from the first time that Jim Gould had seen her, he had been struck by the fact that Cathy Weston was an extremely attractive young woman, but when he picked her up at the Livingstones' house that evening, he realized that she was much more than that. In her crisp white blouse and long black velvet skirt, to his eyes she looked downright beautiful.

'Inspector Weston, you look absolutely stunning.'

His tone was light, but even so, she blushed scarlet. To Cathy's enormous relief he didn't seem to have noticed and opened the car door for her, introducing her to David Harding, who was sitting in the back.

'I'm going to enjoy myself,' she said when they were on their way, 'I've never been to one of these places before.'

'That's the spirit. There's a good deal of drama sometimes; one of the lures of gambling is to stake more than you can afford and our department picks up all sorts of useful tit-bits of information from people who have just won or lost a fortune.'

'I can imagine; perhaps that's how these people managed to get a hold over Bruce.'

'Could be.'

When they arrived, Harding signed them in.

'How much do we owe you for that?'

'Compliments of the department — I'll put it all down to expenses. Hang on here a moment and I'll see if Bruce has arrived yet.'

'Isn't this place out of this world?' said Cathy when Harding had gone. 'I never really believed they existed — just look at the carpet and that chandelier.'

'A place like this just can't lose — it's all a matter of percentages and in any case it's probably as bent as a hair-pin.'

'Not so loud — you'll have us kicked out before we've started. I say, did you see that woman's necklace? If it's real, it must have cost at least five thousand.'

**117**

'We're distinctly out of our league here and no mistake. Ah, here's David.'

'Sorry I've been so long. We're in luck; Bruce is at the roulette table and has evidently been plunging a bit. Do you think he'll recognize you Cathy?'

'I very much doubt it, but I'll keep in the background, just to be on the safe side.'

'No, I didn't mean it that way; I thought if he did, it might soften him up a bit.' He handed her a neat pile of chips. 'Why not join in? You never know, you might win something.'

'But I don't know how to play.'

'There's nothing to it, I'll explain when we go in.'

They went into the smoke filled room. All the seats were taken and they stood some distance behind the players.

'Just watch for a minute or two and you'll see that it's really very simple. The croupier spins the wheel in one direction and throws a small ivory ball in contra-rotation, which, when it slows down sufficiently, falls into one of the numbered compartments.'

'And you place your bets on the similarly numbered squares on the table?'

'Yes, that's right. If you bet on a single number, which is called en plein, the odds are thirty-five to one against. Betting on two numbers simultaneously is called à cheval and you get seventeen to one if either wins. There are all sorts of other combinations, which are a bit too complicated to explain quickly. If I were you, I'd stick to the simple ones and bet on red or black, low, which is one to eighteen, or high, which is nineteen to thirtysix, even or odd. You receive even money on all those. Got the idea?'

'More or less. I'll watch for a bit longer.'

'All right, but be ready to take your place when I give the word; one has to be rather ruthless when the place is as full as this.'

Cathy had picked out Bruce directly she came into the room. He was sitting with a large pile of chips in front of him and it was obvious that he had already had several drinks too many. As she looked on, he began to plunge more and more recklessly and although he won occasionally, his stake money steadily began to dwindle.

A few minutes later, Jim Gould gave Cathy a nudge and pointed to their left. She had no idea how David had known that the woman with the blue rinse was going to vacate her place — to her eye it had looked as if she was settled for the evening — but when she picked up her handbag and edged her seat backwards, he was there to assist her. A large fat man tried to elbow his way through, but found his way blocked by someone even larger. As Cathy slipped into the chair, she heard his voice raised in anger.

'Get out of my way, damn you.'

'Did you speak?'

Cathy saw the man hesitate, but then her view was obstructed and when she looked round again, he was moving away, muttering curses under his breath.

'Mesdames, messieurs, faites vos jeux.'

Across the table, she saw Bruce wipe his damp forehead with a large silk handkerchief and it was immediately obvious to her that he was in such a state that he wouldn't have recognized her even if she had had a placard round her neck. Cathy put a pound on red and watched as the croupier spun the wheel. Apart from an occasional bet at the local point-to-point near her parents' home, she had never gambled in her life and the idea had never held any attraction for her. Now, though, she felt her excitement mounting as the small, ivory ball rattled its way round.

'Rien ne va plus.'

Ten minutes later, she was beginning to see what a fatal fascination the game could have. There was always the temptation to have one more try at recouping one's losses and when a win did come up, it seemed to make up for all the rest. She didn't know how much Bruce had started with, but now he was down to his last four chips. Cathy saw him make a calculation on the note pad beside him and with a shaking hand, he put them all on eighteen. Up to that time, Cathy had not tried a single number herself and put her remaining three pounds on the nearest one to her.

The ball fell into one of the slots with a soft 'clunk' and a fraction of a second before the croupier spoke, she saw all the colour drain from Bruce's face.

'Numéro quinze.'

She watched fascinated, as the man got shakily to his feet and whispered something in the croupier's ear. The man looked over his shoulder, nodded almost imperceptibly and the manager walked across.

'I'm sorry sir, it's a rule of the house.'

'Are you trying to tell me that my cheque's not good enough?'

Bruce's voice had risen and people were beginning to look round, when Harding came up and took his arm.

'Come along Adrian old man, I think I may be able to help you.'

Bruce seemed to see nothing strange in being addressed by a complete stranger and by his christian name at that and allowed himself to be led out of the room. Cathy had been so fascinated by the whole episode, that she had lost track of the game and got to her feet to follow them out.

'Cathy, you idiot,' Jim Gould hissed over her shoulder, 'don't leave your winnings behind.'

The croupier had pushed a great pile of chips across the table towards her with his rake and she gathered them up, blushing scarlet with a mixture of pleasure and embarrassment.

'Never seen anyone in such a hurry to leave when on a winning streak,' said the elderly woman next to her, her Adam's apple bobbing up and down in her scrawny neck.

She went to move to the seat that Cathy had vacated, but was frustrated by the large fat man who subsided into it with a grunt of satisfaction.

'That's my chair,' she shrieked, trying to push him out.

'You seem to have a perfectly good one of your own madam.'

He leaned across her, placed a substantial bet and then sat back, puffing contentedly at his enormous cigar. Cathy would dearly have liked to see the next round of the battle, but Jim was signalling urgently to her from the door.

'Cash those things as quickly as you can; David wants us to have the car ready outside in five minutes time.'

★   ★   ★

'I'm sorry old man, I don't know what this club is coming to — I did my best with that idiot of a manager. I tell you what, come round to my place for a drink — you look as if you could do with one.'

Adrian Bruce didn't know whether he was coming or going. In the previous day or two, he had come to realize exactly to what level he had sunk — he was a drug addict, a thief and now he was involved in a kidnapping. For years, he had pretended to himself that he hadn't known how evil Grey was, but that was the biggest lie of all — he had really been perfectly well aware of it ever since their schooldays together.

There was only one solution and that was to clear out and get himself cured, but to do that, he needed money and plenty of it. But how to get it? His father had long since refused to help him any further and Grey's last payment had not been nearly enough, so with that, and as much as he had been able to borrow from the few friends he still had, he decided to have one last fling at the tables. He had had a series of bad runs and surely his luck would turn soon.

When he got up from the roulette table, Bruce knew utter despair — if only he could have found the courage to do it, he would have ended his misery once and for all. He had gone to pieces so completely that it never occured to him to question the motives of the complete stranger who knew his name. The man was confident, seemed to be in complete control of the situation and was offering him a drink — that was good enough for him.

There was something vaguely familiar about the young woman sitting in the front seat of the car outside; he had thought so before when he had seen her at the roulette table, but for the life of him, he couldn't place her. Bruce began to get uneasy when he was sitting on the back seat next to the confident man, who seemed to have taken over completely and who made no attempt to introduce either himself or the others. He made a half-hearted attempt to get out of the car, but a firm hand pushed him back again.

'I say . . . ' he began, his voice high-pitched with indignation.

'Relax, Adrian old man; you're with friends.' Harding turned and gave him a reassuring smile.

The whole thing was too much for Bruce's drug and alcohol befuddled brain and he settled back uneasily on the seat. The drive took less than twenty minutes, but by the time they had reached Pimlico, Bruce was beginning to sober up. What a fool he had been, he thought, to come with these people. He was somewhat reassured by the presence of the woman — surely she couldn't be anything to do with Grey or the police.

When the car came to a halt, none of them said a word and although the two men didn't lay a hand on him, neither did they leave his side for an instant. They hustled him in through the main entrance of the block of flats and into the lift.

During the short journey upwards, he looked appealingly at the young woman and in the same instant that she turned her head away, he suddenly remembered where he had seen her before and his terror increased still further.

By the time they had reached the apartment, Bruce was stone cold sober and trembling violently.

'Now my friend, you're going to tell us who those people were who got you to switch that brief-case at Waterloo on Thursday.'

'I don't know what you're talking about.'

Bruce licked his lips nervously and made a sudden move towards the door, but abruptly changed his mind when he saw Gould standing right in front of it.

'I think you do,' said Cathy. 'You recognized me in the lift, didn't you?'

It was only too obvious that Bruce had; his mouth dropped open and he subsided into a chair. Harding gripped him by the lapels of his coat and jerked him upright.

'Take off your coat and shirt.'

'What the hell do . . . '

'Shut up! Look, if you don't take them off yourself, we'll do it for you. Take your choice.'

Harding drew back his fist and Bruce flinched as if he had been struck already, then slowly began to undo the buttons on his jacket.

'So the rumours were true; that explains a lot.'

The man's upper arms were pitted with needle marks and on the left, a thrombosed vein snaked its way up his forearm.

'He's obviously been at it for years, main-lining too. What are you on Bruce? Heroin?'

The man pulled his arm away, shook his head violently and began to put his shirt back on.

'It was your drug suppliers who made you do it, wasn't it?' Bruce stood in the middle of the floor, glancing this way and that like a hunted animal. 'Now look here, a couple have had their baby kidnapped and you helped the people responsible to get away with the money.'

'You can't prove it.'

'I don't need to. I can't think why I should go to the trouble, and you certainly don't deserve it, but I'll do a deal with you. Tell me exactly what happened, who supplies you with the drugs and I'll arrange for you to go somewhere to get treatment.'

'Who are you?' Bruce's face was the colour of putty.

'I'm a mean bastard, that's what I am and just how mean, you're very soon going to find out unless you start talking.'

'They'll kill me.'

'There are many ways of dying, my dear fellow, and by the time I've finished with you, you'll be begging me to complete the job. You may not believe this, but some people actually enjoy inflicting pain and I'm one of them.'

Bruce's head sagged forward on his chest. 'All right,' he said almost inaudibly.

Harding turned towards Gould and pursed his lips in a gesture of relief.

'Stop him!' Cathy shouted suddenly.

Harding whirled round, but he was too late; Bruce projected himself at the window and just short of it, took off in a flat dive. There was a splintering crash of breaking glass, the man let out a despairing shout and then disappeared from view. They all heard the cry abruptly cut off and the sickening thud as he hit the ground twenty feet below. For a moment, all three of them stood there motionless, appalled by what had happened, then the spell was broken and Harding made a dash for the door and the others followed him down the stairs as fast as they could.

Bruce was lying huddled up on the ground, one leg twisted at an unnatural angle, but when Cathy knelt beside him, she was relieved to find that he was still breathing and that his pulse was quite strong.

'What do you think Cathy?'

'He's still alive, but I can't see how badly hurt he is yet, although he's obviously fractured his leg. David, would you ring for an ambulance and bring a torch down with you?'

Lights had sprung up all over the block of flats, several people were hanging out of the windows and when she looked over her shoulder, she saw a couple wearing dressing-gowns coming out of the front entrance.

'Jim, can you try to keep the ghouls at bay?'

'Right.' He strode across the lawn. 'It's all right everybody — there's been an accident, but the man's not seriously hurt. There's a doctor with him and the ambulance will be here shortly.'

'That's all very well, young man, but what are you doing here? I know everyone in this block of flats and I've never seen you before.'

The peppery looking man with the grey moustache only came up to Gould's shoulder, but he did not appear in the least bit daunted. By this time, about fifteen people had collected in a group on the steps.

'Quite right Colonel,' said a woman wearing a hair-net, 'shall I send for the police?'

'I've already done so.' Harding's confident figure appeared at the front door. 'Ah, Colonel Forsythe, just the man I was looking for. May I have a private word with you?' He gave Gould a wink and after handing him the torch, took the Colonel by the arm and out of ear-shot of the others. 'Bad business this sir; fact is that I brought my two friends back for a night-cap and we caught this chap burgling the flat. Fellow panicked and threw himself out of the window — seemed half crazy, probably on drugs if the truth be known.' He glanced back towards the others. 'You know these people here better than anyone, do you think you could calm them down — I wouldn't want them to think that there were thieves about.'

'Leave it to me, young fellow. Can't have the women-folk gettin' in a state.'

By the time Harding had rejoined the others, they could hear the little man barking out commands and slowly the crowd dispersed and the heads disappeared from the windows.

'How did you work that miracle?' asked Gould.

'The gallant colonel's in his element when ordering people about — normally he's only got his wife and dachshund to practise on and she's almost stone deaf and the dog takes not a blind bit of notice. Something like this is right up his street, particularly as I think he suspects that I'm in the intelligence service.' He went down on one knee. 'How's Bruce?'

'Not too bad fortunately. As I suspected, his leg's gone, but he's not deeply unconscious — it was very lucky that he landed on the grass.'

Although they were dressed in the correct uniform, Cathy thought there was something distinctly odd about the ambulance men directly they appeared, Bruce being put on a stretcher and carried away without either of them uttering a single word. Harding motioned to Gould and Cathy and they all got into the back, but it was not until the vehicle was on the move that he said anything.

'You've probably guessed that this ambulance belongs to the department — I was thinking that it might be safer if we took Bruce out of circulation for a bit. He must be more deeply involved in this whole business than I realized to have reacted in the way he did and we don't want the opposition to know what's happened to him. In a minor way he's quite a security risk too.'

'There's something that's been worrying me,' said Cathy. 'Suppose that the people who run the gambling club are connected with the kidnapping; they'll know that we took Bruce away and they'll be even more suspicious if he disappears without any explanation.'

'I shouldn't concern yourself too much about that. I'm fairly well known at the club and I told the manager I was at school with Bruce and suggested that I took him off their hands before he created a disturbance. The man seemed only too pleased with the idea, but nevertheless I think you've got a point. Why don't I have it put around that Bruce attempted suicide and his father had him admitted to a private mental hospital.'

'Where had you in mind?' asked Gould.

'We run a place in Hertfordshire for just this type of emergency, which is thought to be one by the locals. That's how I came to think of the idea.'

'That's all very well David; heaven knows, I'm no doctor, but I'm sure he's going to need major surgery to that leg and I think he may have broken some ribs as well — suppose he were to die on the way there?'

'Hmm, you've got a point there; I think you're right, it would be too far. Why not let us get him patched up at St Gregory's Hospital? I know the doctor in charge of the Intensive Care Unit there and he could be transferred to our place as soon as he's fit enough.'

'What about security at the hospital?'

'I don't think that should be any problem.'

'I'd certainly be much happier with that arrangement,' said Cathy.

'When do you think he'll be fit enough for questioning?' asked Gould. 'He is after all our only lead.'

'I've no idea; we'll have to ask Dr Beck when we get there.'

Cathy was surprised to find that not only was Dr Beck a woman, but a very attractive one too. As she watched them together, it was also perfectly obvious to her that the blonde young woman and Harding were more than just friends. What was the matter with her? Why didn't men like Harding look at her like that? Why did it always have to be people like that awful Ferguson in the forensic laboratory who seemed interested in her? She sighed deeply and Gould rested his hand briefly on hers.

'Don't worry, it couldn't be helped and at least Bruce will be quite safe here.'

Cathy flushed slightly, making a firm resolution to keep her mind more firmly on the job in hand and at the same time realizing the illogicality of her thoughts; the fault was entirely hers really, someone like Gould had only to make one friendly gesture and she shied away like a frightened pony.

'I'm still concerned that the kidnappers will find out what has happened to him.'

They had to wait for nearly an hour before Dr Beck and the orthopaedic surgeon came out of the cubicle.

'What's the verdict?'

'None too good, I'm afraid. He's going to need a tracheotomy — his breathing's not adequate — and surgery to that leg tonight. He's not deeply unconscious, but I doubt if you'll get anything useful out of him for a day or two at best.'

'Well, I suppose we must be grateful that he's still alive,' said Harding. 'Do you mind if we keep one of our men in his room the whole time?'

'Not at all; we've had prisoners with guards in here before. Sister Agnew's not going to like it, but I expect I'll be able to talk her round.'

Harding was not entirely happy with the arrangement, but was somewhat reassured when he had inspected the lay-out of the unit more carefully. It was at the end of a separate corridor, the staff were all specially trained and the chance of anyone being able to get at Bruce seemed remote in the extreme.

After thanking Dr Beck, all three of them went back to the Livingstones' house.

'Don't bother to get out,' said Cathy as the car drew up outside, 'I can manage.'

'That's all right, I wanted to have a word with the constable on duty outside anyway.'

Harding looked out of the car window with an amused smile on his face as the two of them went up the steps and into the hall; watching them throughout the evening had made him feel quite old.

'I'm so glad you came Cathy. I'm very sorry about Bruce, but it was rather fun in that club, wan't it? How much did you win?'

Cathy's hand flew to her mouth. 'How awful of me! I haven't even counted it, let alone paid David back.' She took the bundle of notes out of her bag and flicked them through quickly. 'It's over £1000. Jim, would you give it back to him? . . . Please.'

'Don't be such a goose. I'll give him the £10 stake money, but not a penny more. Good night, sleep well.'

Before she could move, he kissed her quickly on the lips and was gone before she could say anything further. Cathy stood for a long time in the hall, then as she slowly climbed the narrow staircase, a tear made its way down her cheek.

# 6

'Yes Andrews, what is it?'

'It's Bruce; there's been some trouble at the casino.'

Grey listened in silence until the man had finished. 'I'll be over in five minutes.'

He put down the telephone and sat for a moment at the desk, gently tapping the blotter with an ornate paper knife — perhaps it had not been such a good idea to use Bruce after all.

Andrews was setting up the video-tape machine when he arrived and he watched intently as the recording was played back.

'Hold it! Who's that man?'

He narrowed his eyes and peered intently at the rather fuzzy picture on the screen.

'Bloke by the name of Harding; he's been a member of the club for a year or two now.'

'What does he do?'

'Said to work for an import-export

firm. He doesn't spend all that much, but he comes here quite a lot. Oh, there was one other thing — he told me that he had been at school with Bruce, that was the reason he gave for having an interest in him.'

'Did he now? Well, apart from anything else, our friend Harding is a liar. What about the couple?'

Andrews pressed a button and they watched the two of them chatting together in the foyer of the club. 'Never seen them before — they signed in as a Mr and Mrs Bishop.'

'Is Mulligan in the building?' The other man nodded. 'Send him up right away, will you?'

Mulligan needed only one quick glance at the screen. 'It's her all right — the Livingstone woman. I was quite close to her at the station and I've no doubt about it.'

'Just as I thought.'

'Do you want us to go ahead as planned tomorrow, boss?'

'I'll let you know later. Andrews, get me Harding's address, and Mulligan, you bring the car round to the front right away.'

★ ★ ★

As soon as they had driven round the corner, Grey could see that something out of the ordinary had happened. Although it was nearly midnight, several people were standing on the pavement looking over the fence and as he got out of the car, he heard shouts coming from the entrance to the block of flats.

Grey went up to a young man who was holding a Dalmation on a lead. 'What's up?'

'I gather that some chap threw himself out of that first floor window. I was up the road when I heard the glass go and when I got here, some people were already seeing to him.'

'Is he dead?'

'I don't know, but even if he's not, he must be pretty badly hurt. He hasn't moved in all the time I've been watching.'

Grey could just make out the figure lying on the grass with the woman kneeling beside him and saw that the end of the building was only ten feet from them.

'I'll see if I can do anything to help — I'm a doctor.'

He sprinted down the road and up the drive towards the main entrance to the block of flats. Ten minutes later, the ambulance arrived and soon after Grey slipped into the back seat of the Jaguar.

'Follow that ambulance when it comes out,' he said, 'but be careful how you do it.'

On the journey, Grey sat silent, deep in thought. He had managed to get close enough to the group on the grass to hear that it definitely was Bruce, that he was not too badly hurt and that Harding was involved with the intelligence services. He thought it improbable that Bruce had talked, but how long that desirable state of affairs would last was quite another matter; the security people could be a ruthless lot of bastards and he knew from long experience that the man was as weak as water. It was absolutely typical of him to have proved incapable of making an efficient job even of killing himself.

It had always been the same and Grey cast his mind back to the time when they had been at public school together. Bruce's father, Lord Minter, never refused him anything and Grey never had understood how a man known for his ruthless financial decisions and lack of sentimentality, could be so weak where his son was concerned.

Grey's parents had split up years earlier and although his education was being paid for by a trust fund, he was given very little pocket money. The arrangement did not suit him at all well — he had a girl down in the town who used to cost him a small fortune and when the worst happened and she got pregnant, he suddenly found himself having to face the prospect of getting hold of £100 or having the whole thing discovered and being expelled for a certainty. Although in many ways he would have been delighted to have seen the back of the place, it would have meant that his chances of going to university and medical school would be finished for ever.

Bruce was the obvious and indeed the only person who might have access to as large a sum as that, indeed in the past he had been able to touch the boy, who was a year his junior, for various small sums. Grey thought long and hard about the best way of getting him to part with it and the opportunity arose one day when he heard screams of terror coming from outside the house. Bruce was hanging upside down from a third storey window, suspended by two sheets which had been knotted together and tied to one of his ankles. When Grey rushed out, he saw that the other end of the sheet must have been secured to something inside the dormitory, because Fraser, who had always made the other boy's life an utter misery, was leaning out of the window, pulling on the sheet and making Bruce swing in a wide arc like a gigantic pendulum. Later that day, Grey went along to the younger boy's study.

'How much would you give me if I stopped Fraser from bullying you for ever?'

'I'd give you anything.'

'£100?'

'I'd even give you that much if I had it.'

'You could get if from your father if you really tried — ask him for a hi-fi set or something. I wouldn't expect you to pay until you had seen some results.'

Bruce had thought about it for a day or two and then agreed. He didn't see what Grey would be able to do, but it was quite true that it wouldn't be difficult to work on his father and anything would be better than having to put up with a repetition of his terrifying experience of that terrible afternoon. He was in mortal terror of Fraser and had even thought of killing himself in order to escape the tyranny to which he was constantly subjected.

Within a fortnight Fraser was stricken by a mysterious illness; he lost weight, he developed terrible abdominal colic and couldn't stop vomiting. Several doctors came to see him, he was transferred to the local hospital, he even had an exploratory operation, but was all to no avail; ten days later, Fraser died.

Their house-master hadn't realized that

Grey and the sick boy were so friendly and in any case it surprised him to see how upset he seemed to be and how often he asked to see Fraser. Nevertheless, he thought it would be a mistake to discourage a show of emotion in a boy he had always thought to be cold and calculating and so he allowed him to go to the hospital as often as he wished.

Bruce handed over the money a week or two later.

'I say Grey, you didn't . . . I mean Fraser's illness was just a coincidence wasn't it?'

'My dear fellow, what are you trying to suggest? I was just lucky, that's all.'

The incident had taught Grey several things; he could twist Bruce round his little finger, there was a great deal of money to be made out of illegal abortions and even an elementary knowledge of drugs and poisons, even those available in the school chemistry laboratory, was a very powerful weapon. He had not in fact meant to kill Fraser, but now that he had done so, he did not feel the slightest remorse, rather a sense of power.

Grey's assiduous cultivation of Bruce after this incident continued to reap dividends. In the normal course of events, his exam results would not have been good enough to get him into medical school, but Lord Minter was on the board of governors of one of the London teaching hospitals and that was sufficient.

At first, all had gone well with Grey at medical school and the fact that he had lost contact with Bruce, who had gone to Washington with his father, did not worry him at all. As he had suspected, the illegal abortion business was a prosperous one and with the money that that provided, he enjoyed the life enormously. In fact, he was the envy of the others; he always seemed to have a different girl in tow and the means to entertain them in a style that none of the other students could match.

This highly desirable existence as far as he was concerned came to an abrupt halt one day when one of his 'patients', who happened to be a nurse at the hospital, developed a severe haemorrhage after his ministrations and had to be admitted to the gynaecological ward. Grey was extremely lucky not to have been prosecuted — it was only the fear of unsavoury publicity on the part of the hospital authorities that saved him — but he was thrown out of the medical school.

The situation did not trouble him unduly, for, in a quiet way he had been preparing for it. He had long since decided that there was not nearly enough money or scope for his talents in medicine and he had been making discreet contacts. It had also been clear to him for some time that once the law was reformed, the bottom would drop out of the illegal abortion business, apart from the fact that it was risky and he was proposing to set his sights much higher.

Grey soon found that he didn't have enough capital to make the sort of start he needed and it was not long before his thoughts once again turned in Bruce's direction. He discovered that his school-friend had returned from the States, was working in the civil service and most important of all, had come into some money on reaching his majority.

Grey hadn't lost his ability to influence the younger man and had no difficulty in getting a loan from him. His first club was a success and within two years he was able to pay back the money. His formula was a simple one; most of the girls he employed as hostesses were just out of prison and he gave them good accommodation, paid them well, looked after their medical care and gave them a percentage of the earnings they only too easily made outside 'normal' business hours. If a girl wanted to leave, he never put pressure on her to stay and word soon got around that he treated them fairly; as a result, he was never short of replacements. Only once had a girl tried to cheat him and then he had gathered them all together, explained that the system would only work if there was mutual trust on both sides and invited them to deal with her themselves. Even he was shaken by what they did to her, but he never had any trouble again.

Grey soon acquired another club and as his sphere of influence increased, so did his need to protect himself from some of the mobsters, who saw him as a threat to their empires. After a year or two, they found that both he and the men he employed were utterly ruthless; one of their number was heard to boast about what he was going to do to Grey and when, soon after, the man was found floating in the Thames, the others took the hint and left him strictly alone.

Grey had been thinking of going into the gambling business for some time and when Bruce came to see him one day it was just the stimulus he needed. The man was obviously ill; he had lost weight, his complexion was sallow and he seemed to have aged ten years since Grey had seen him last. It did not take long for the story to come out; Bruce had started to gamble, had been introduced to drugs and was now being bled dry by Daniel Weiss, the man who ran the club to which he belonged. Even his father had rebelled in the end and had refused to let him have any more money.

Grey did not feel in the least sorry for the man — he was quite uncapable of such an emotion — but he did see it as a way of acquiring a new business interest and it would certainly do no harm to keep in with him. Lord Minter was still an important man and apart from the obvious blackmailing possibilities, it would certainly be valuable to have friends in high places.

Daniel Weiss had heard about Grey and didn't trust him an inch, but he never refused the opportunity of a good meal, let alone one at the best restaurant in London, particularly if someone else was paying for it. In addition to his notorious meanness, he was by nature a suspicious man, but he was also vain and even began to relax and enjoy himself when Grey told him that he was thinking of starting a gambling club in Sardinia and wanted his advice about the best way to go about it.

A short time later, Weiss developed a gastric upset. At first, it was put down to a virus illness, but he steadily got worse and lapsed into coma. It was only then that he was admitted to hospital and the correct diagnosis made, but it was far too late. His death caused a considerable stir in medical circles — the man had not been abroad for many years and deaths from typhoid in London were a rare occurrence indeed.

Grey had gone to a good deal of trouble and expense to get hold of the culture, but it had been worthwhile; he knew that Bruce would never have accepted a second totally unexplained death and when the cause was published in the newspapers, as he had hoped, the man put it down to a fortunate coincidence.

With his family connections and social contacts, Bruce continued to be useful. He had an entrée to many country houses and on a number of occasions was the inside man for a series of robberies that was part of Grey's new field of activity, which also included Weiss' gambling club. He had also moved into the drugs racket and kept Bruce under his thumb by supplying him with heroin and allowing him to win small sums at the roulette table. But now, he thought, as he watched the ambulance turn in through the main gates of St Gregory's Hospital, Bruce had become a major liability; the man had become totally unbalanced, he knew too much and he was going to have to go.

* ★ *

Sister Agnew was in a bad mood; the management of patients was quite difficult enough without having to put up with large policemen sitting in their rooms and getting in the way. She snatched up the phone directly it began to ring.

'Intensive Care Unit — Sister Agnew speaking,' she snapped.

'One moment please, I have Mr Laurence Braithwaite on the line for you.'

'Ah Sister, good morning. I am ringing to ask if it would be convenient for me to call in to see Mr Bruce in about half an hour's time. Lord Minter has asked for a second opinion and Dr Beck telephoned me about it a short while ago.'

'Yes, that would be quite all right sir. I'm afraid that Dr Beck won't be here to meet you — she's attending a meeting in Birmingham today.'

'Yes I know, she told me.'

'I'll get the senior registrar to wait for you in the front hall.'

'Please don't worry Sister; I hate these

153

committee style consultations. I'll find my own way up and have a word with him afterwards. And how is the patient?'

'He's conscious, but still pretty weak.'

Sister Agnew was a nurse of the old school; she liked consultants to look like consultants and in Mr Laurence Braithwaite she was not disappointed. What a pity, she thought, when he came in, that so few of them seemed to dress the part these days; the surgeon looked so distinguished in his immaculate black coat and striped trousers. Young he may have been, but there was no mistaking his confidence and authority.

'Would you like to see the patient first, Mr Braithwaite, or would you prefer to study the notes and X-rays?'

'The notes first, the patient next and finally the X-rays, I think Sister, thank you.'

Grey scanned the folder quickly and gave a grunt of satisfaction when he saw the extent of the man's injuries and the fact that they had carried out a tracheotomy on him. If conscious, Bruce was bound to recognize him, but with a tube in his throat, there wouldn't be much he could do about it. It should be a piece of cake.

His confidence took a sharp dip when he was shown into the side room and saw the man sitting on a chair at the foot of the bed and although he got to his feet, he showed absolutely no sign of going.

'Would you leave us please?'

'I'm sorry Sister, but you know that my orders were most particular and you'll remember that Dr Beck did agree.'

Grey did not in the least like the look of the young man in the lounge suit — he knew instinctively that he was not the sort of person who could be bullied or browbeaten.

'This really is most irregular Sister — indeed I cannot recall a similar incident — but still, it is the patient who is the most important person after all and one cannot afford to be too sensitive these days.'

'Would you please move right out of the way?'

Sister Agnew shooed the young man into a corner. She wouldn't have blamed

Mr Braithwaite if he had walked straight out; she did not approve of having a guard put on Bruce and had no intention of letting him get in the way.

Grey was thinking furiously as he looked down at the man on the bed. He had anticipated having to get rid of the ward sister for a minute or two, but now there seemed no chance at all of being left alone. Bruce had not seen him yet; he was lying flat on his back, breathing noisily though the tracheotomy tube. His chest was swathed in bandages, his right arm was in plaster and traction was being applied to his left leg by means of heavy weights at the foot of the bed.

'Mr Bruce? Mr Bruce, can you hear me? There's a surgeon come to see you — a Mr Braithwaite.'

Grey saw the man's eyelids flick open and then the expression of horror as he recognized who it was. Bruce thrashed his head from side to side and tried desperately to speak, but merely produced a whistling breath through the tube. Grey placed himself firmly beween the guard and the injured man, put his medical bag on the bedside table and bent over it. When he straightened up, he had the full syringe hidden in his left hand and his ophthalmoscope in his right.

'I'm so sorry Sister, I wonder if I could trouble you for another instrument; the bulb seems to have gone in mine and I don't have a spare.'

'Of course, I'll get it right away.'

The minute she had gone, Grey turned towards the guard. 'There's rather too much light in here for me to use the ophthalmoscope properly and I'd be greatly obliged if you'd pull the curtain across for me.'

Bruce was covered by a single sheet and Grey was able to make out the contour of his right thigh. With one decisive movement, he stabbed the needle straight through the sheet and pressed the plunger home, at the same time leaning on the man's leg with his full weight to prevent him from kicking. The precaution was hardly necessary; Bruce was so weak that he hardly moved.

By the time the guard had turned

round again, the syringe and needle were safely in Grey's pocket and he smiled warmly at the man.

'Thank you so much. It must get pretty tedious for you here, I imagine . . . Ah Sister, thank you.'

Grey took his time over the examination and when he had finished, washed his hands and studied the X-rays on the viewing box in the room until he was satisfied that the drug would have had time to work. He had given Bruce a simply enormous dose of heroin, but the man was used to it and he knew what a tolerance addicts could develop.

'Good-bye, my dear fellow. We won't be seeing one another again, but I can certainly reassure your father that you are in the very best of hands.'

Bruce's lips moved feebly and he looked with mute appeal towards the Sister.

'Try to get some sleep now Mr Bruce.'

Grey nodded to the guard and as he left the room, saw the man settle back in his chair.

'Well, thank you very much Sister. You run a most efficient unit, if I may say so.'

The woman flushed with pleasure. 'Let me ring the senior registrar for you sir.'

'Perhaps it would be more courteous if I telephoned Dr Beck tonight when she gets back. I will of course be sending her a letter in due course.'

'Won't you stay for a cup of coffee sir?'

Grey glanced at his watch. 'You tempt me sorely Sister, but I'm afraid that I must be on my way.'

It took all of his considerable self-control to prevent himself from running out of the hospital, but he forced himself to walk through the front hall at a steady pace. Mulligan, in a chauffeur's uniform, was waiting for him outside in the BMW and he leaned back on the rear seat, feeling the sweat running down the inside of his shirt.

# 7

Livingstone seemed to be a changed man when Cathy came down to breakfast the following morning; he looked as if he had had a good night's sleep and his manner was much more relaxed and natural.

'I don't think I can stand hanging about here all day,' he said when they had finished their meal. 'I was thinking of going down to Henley to put in some work on the cabin cruiser we have there. Care to come with me?'

It was the first friendly approach he had made and Cathy only took a moment to make up her mind.

'I'd love to; I could do with a day off myself. I'd just better ring the Yard to make sure that nothing has cropped up.'

Once she had heard that Bruce was not expected to be fit enough to talk that day, Cathy decided to do her best to forget about the whole wretched business and enjoy herself. Livingstone seemed equally determined to make a success of the day; he lent her one of his wife's bathing costumes, helped her to get a picnic lunch together and on the way to the mooring, kept her entertained with stories about some of his more eccentric clients.

'Well, here we are,' he said as they turned down a narrow track short of the town.

For the next few minutes he was busy taking the cover off the cockpit of the cabin cruiser and when he had finished, he looked up at the cloudless blue sky.

'To hell with tarting the old girl up,' he said, 'this isn't the sort of day for scraping and painting. Let's go for a trip, shall we?'

He filled the boat up with petrol and they went slowly up-stream, Livingstone standing behind the wheel, puffing contentedly at his pipe, while Cathy sat on the roof of the cabin in her bathing costume, watching the river traffic and enjoying the feel of the hot sun on her shoulders.

'Is this where they hold the Royal Regatta?'

'Yes, that's right. The Leander Club's over there.'

161

'I've never been to it — it all looks marvellously pre-war from the photographs, I must say.'

Livingstone laughed. 'It really is just like that and class-ridden through and through; that's a good part of the fascination, all those old boys in their yellow flannels and faded caps. Still, rowing in it must count as one of the greatest thrills in my life. There are lots of people who can't see anything in rowing at all, but they've never known what it's like to be in an eight that's really on song and see the opposition gradually slipping back inch by inch; it can be sheer poetry.'

Livingstone found a convenient landing place and they spread out a rug on the grassy bank.

'I wasn't going to bring up the subject of the other night again,' he said after they had had lunch and were sunbathing, 'but if you're going to go on living in my house with any confidence, I've decided that I must. Don't think that I'm going to start making excuses, because there aren't any but I would like to try to explain.'

The fact that she was three feet away

from him and that, lying on his back he couldn't see her, somehow made it so much easier for him. He told her about his life with Mary, how it had all changed after Mark's birth and how finally he had come to wish that she would die, something he had hardly admitted to himself.

'We had been so happy — you know, physically — but all that stopped, just like that. When she was at home, Mary spent her whole time staring into space or even worse, crying and self-recriminating, that is if she wasn't flattened by drugs or confused by electrical treatment. What happened to Mark nearly finished me completely, but it was your arrival that was the last straw. The trouble was that you really are rather like Mary in many ways and the thought of you up there was too much for me. I got drunk and you know the rest.' He picked the petals carefully off a daisy. 'It can't have been easy for you to have stayed on after that, let alone come out with me today and I just wanted you to know that I do appreciate your trust and all that you are doing to help us.' He reached out for her hand and gripped it gently and then more firmly when she tried to draw it away. 'You're not still scared of me are you?'

Cathy smiled nervously. 'A bit, but it's not only that — I have this stupid thing about being touched.'

He didn't let her go and she didn't have the courage to pull her hand right away.

'There's nothing wrong with touching, you know; I sometimes think that many people these days have completely lost the art of it. To touch is to be in contact with a fellow human, to support the person your are touching, and I am in desperate need of that. Do you know why I asked you out today?' Cathy shook her head. 'Well, there were several reasons — I felt that both of us were in need of a break, I wanted to try to make up for the other night and from a purely selfish point of view, I urgently required help. I was abrupt and rude when we first met and then saw how you shied away from me later and how frightened of me you were. You may not believe this, but I'm not really like that at all. I'm the sort of man who needs a woman, a woman both to talk to and confide in and when I saw that I had caused you to reject me in that way, I drank too much and went temporarily mad. You are a beautiful and attractive girl and this afternoon is the one time in months that I have felt even remotely at peace. I want to be near to you and to hold you for a little time, nothing more than that, and you have nothing to fear from me, I promise you.'

No one had ever spoken to Cathy like that and she felt the tears coming to her eyes. When he pulled her towards him, she didn't resist and gradually began to relax as she lay with her head on his chest while he gently stroked her cheek. She found herself telling him things she had never dreamed of telling anyone before, her fears of men and sex, her dislike of the coarse jokes and the way the others treated her and finally her worry that there was something seriously wrong with her.

He listened in silence until she had finished.

'You poor old thing — you should have told someone about all this years ago. Do you know what President Roosevelt said at the time of his first inaugural address in 1933 at the time of the great depression? He said; 'the only thing we have to fear is fear itself.' Exactly the same thing could be said of you. Sex can be serious, but it can be fun too; if you aren't shocked by the remarks the others make and the jokes they tell, they'll soon stop trying to shock you. You must know better than me that many rape victims bring the situation on themselves; believe me, I'm not trying to excuse myself, but if, right from the start you hadn't behaved as if I was about to attack you at any moment, I doubt if the idea would have entered my head. I even saw it in the way you behaved with that chap Gould last night. He obviously finds you attractive and enjoys looking at you; what's wrong with that? You're worth looking at. Perhaps it's not for me to say, but instead of giving him the old refrigeration treatment and being scared, you ought to be flattered, he's a nice looking fellow.'

Cathy told him about the 'check-up' joke and he roared with laughter. After a moment, she began to get the giggles herself.

'In fact, it is quite funny when I think about it now and yet I was both furious and disgusted at the time.'

'You're learning.'

'Well, that's enough of my trouble. And to think that you asked me to give you support.'

'You've been more help than you'll ever know. What about a swim? I'm being roasted alive.'

Cathy could hardly believe it all when she sat with her legs dangling over the side of the boat when they were on their way back. She had actually been in physical contact with a man for a whole hour and enjoyed it. She had let herself go and unburdened herself to someone for the first time in her life and could still feel the relief. She had also fooled around with him in the water and been none too gently spanked for ducking him and she had even enjoyed that. As she turned to watch him standing massively behind the wheel, she couldn't imagine how she had ever thought him frightening. The day before, the smile he gave her would no doubt have provoked blushing embarrassment, but now, as she returned it, she felt a quite different emotion.

As they had arranged, Cathy rang Jim Gould as soon as they got back to Chelsea.

'I'm afraid that Bruce died late this morning,' he said, distress in his voice obvious.

'But they told me at the hospital that he was doing quite well. What happened?'

'He was got at.'

'What! But how?'

'An orthopaedic surgeon called Lawrence Braithwaite came to see him at ten o'clock and he died forty-five minutes later.'

'But what has that got to do with it?'

'Only that the real Mr Braithwaite is on a lecture tour in India. Whoever impersonated him must have discovered that Dr Beck was away for the day and told the ward sister that he had been called in by Bruce's father for a second opinion.'

'But how did he manage to kill him? I thought the guard was under orders not

to leave the room under any circumstances.'

'You're quite right and he didn't. We
don't know how it was done yet, but I
personally have no doubts that his death
wasn't due to natural causes — that
would have been a quite absurd coincidence.'

'Did you get a useful description of the
bogus surgeon?'

'Yes, pretty good in fact — luckily the
guard was an excellent observer. We're
getting an artist on to it. How are things
your end?'

'Much better, I'm glad to say. Livingstone's a really nice bloke once you get to
know him.'

*　*　*

The telephone rang again at four o'clock
the following morning and Cathy recognized the voice at once.

'You shouldn't have let the police try to
set up a trap you know, you really
shouldn't. It's lucky for you that I was in
a good mood otherwise it might really

169

have been your son's foot. I've decided that you've been taught a severe enough lesson and that you may collect the boy tonight.'

'Is Mark all right?'

'Be quiet and listen. Don't leave the house all day; we will be watching and if you try any further tricks I won't be so lenient. At exactly eleven o'clock tonight you will leave in your car and drive to the access road outside Waterloo Station; go to the same telephone booth as before and await further instructions. I don't imagine that I need warn you again of the consequences of any stupidity on your part.'

John Livingstone met her on the stairs after the man had rung off and they both went back to the double bedroom.

'I can't ask you to do any more,' he said. 'In any case, I don't believe they intend to hand Mark over at all; they obviously just want to make things as wretched as possible for us and Mary in particular. Why else would they be going to all this trouble?'

'We can't give up now.'

'Perhaps not, but I'm going to be the one to go.'

'But you heard what they said and if I have the two-way radio, it won't be all that risky.'

'I realize that, but if your safety is really looked after, there'll be a good chance that the kidnappers will know that you're being shadowed.'

They talked it over it for more than an hour and finally agreed to leave the final decision until they had had a chance to discuss it with Gould and Harding. They had been sitting side by side on the bed and when Livingstone put his arm round her shoulders, she didn't even have to resist the impulse to draw away — there wasn't one.

'What was that about Mark's foot,' he said after a long silence. Cathy told him in detail. 'It was very thoughtful of you to have protected me from it, particularly after the way I had behaved, but you won't need to do it again whatever happens — I can take anything now.'

'I know.'

Cathy wasn't sure who made the first

move, but as if it had been the most natural thing in the world, they got under the bed clothes and soon fell asleep in each other's arms.

* ★ ★

If they had not been forced to discuss the situation over the telephone, Cathy doubted if the three of them would have been able to persuade John Livingstone to accept their plan. In the end though, he did agree, but only on condition that he joined one of the three support cars.

During the afternoon, the constable who had come to take up duty outside, delivered some fresh equipment and after that, it was just a question of sitting out the time. Earlier, John Livingstone had gone out to join Harding and the last four hours sitting alone dragged by interminably. At last it was eleven o'clock and she was able to leave. She was wearing the same microphone round her neck, but they had increased the power of the batteries, which she was now carrying, together with the rest of the apparatus, in

172

a special belt around her waist, the whole being hidden by her voluminous jumper. Both the reception and the range were much improved and her confidence was further boosted by the homing device in the heel of her left shoe.

Jim Gould had asked her to give a continuous running commentary, unless it seemed likely to make her conspicuous when other people were around and she started directly she left the house.

'I am closing the front door now. There is a couple walking past on the other side of the road, but no one else is in sight. I am now getting into the car and have checked to see that the boot is still locked and that nothing has been put inside.'

Cathy kept it up all the way to the station. Although she presumed that her journey was being covered by her colleagues and she kept a close look-out, she never once saw them and could have sworn that she was not being followed by anyone else.

At that time of night, there was very little traffic about and she arrived at her destination at twenty past eleven. She walked into the station fore-court and as she approached the telephone box, looked round to make sure that no one was within earshot.

'I don't see anyone suspicious; I'm going to go up to the booth.' She inspected the apparatus carefully. 'There doesn't seem to be any message here.'

'Don't worry, we are close at hand.'

Cathy gave a sudden start when the telephone bell rang and she snatched up the receiver.

'Go back to your car and look under the back wheels.'

There was a click and then the dialling tone. Cathy walked back to the parking area and on the ground, beneath the silencer, she found an envelope. She got into the car, switched on the interior light and read out the contents of the letter over the transmitter.

'Did you see who put it there?'

'No, we had a man watching your car, but he was not able to get too close without making it too obvious and in any case, his view was constantly being obstructed by passing vehicles. Someone probably crawled along behind the row of parked cars.'

'Shall I carry out their instructions?'

'Yes, we know where the place is. Don't drive too quickly — we are sending one of our cars off ahead of you.'

The directions on the typed sheet were quite clear, but once in the Wapping area, Cathy had no clear idea of where she was. Eventually she arrived in the correct road and found a further envelope attached to one of the lamp-posts. Although she could have read the message perfectly well outside, she got back into the car and leaned over the passenger seat so that anyone watching would be unable to see her lips moving.

'It's not going to be all that easy. It's so quiet outside that if anyone is close by in one of these houses, they're bound to hear me speaking on the radio. I'll read out the instructions now and when I am about to enter the house, I'll give a cough.'

'Right,' came the reply. 'We'll only speak to you in an emergency. You can start now.'

Cathy took a torch out of the glove compartment and set off. She had to walk about a mile; she had not been given the street names, just the turns to make and after about fifteen minutes, she reached a dingy side road. Number forty-three was like all the other smoke blackened terrace houses, which all looked as if they were scheduled for destruction, the majority being already unoccupied and many having boarded-up windows.

Hesitantly, Cathy walked up the weed covered path and stood at the front door, her heart pounding like a steam hammer. She gave it a tentative push and to her surprise it swung open easily and after giving a loud cough, she stepped over the threshold.

The narrow entrance hall was dusty, the linoleum had been half ripped away from the rotten floor-boards and as she swung the beam of the torch round, she could see great patches of damp on the plaster where the wall paper had come away. She flicked the light switch on and off a couple of times, but as she had expected, the electricity had been disconnected.

There were three doors leading off the hall, but she ignored them when she saw the arrow which had been roughly drawn on a piece of paper and stuck to the banisters with a drawing pin. The deathly silence was beginning to play on her nerves and she was only just able to resist the temptation to speak on the radio. She bolstered up her courage by stamping up the stairs and hoped that the listening police would realize what she was doing.

On the landing at the top, she found another arrow pointing towards the rear bedroom. All the way up she had been aware of the nauseating smell, which became stronger as she climbed higher and when she pushed open the door with her foot, it hit her with full force. The room was empty apart from a bundle in one corner, which was covered with sacking and was obviously the source of the smell. Cathy was almost paralysed with horror, but she just had to know and before she had too much time to think, she rushed across the room and snatched the covering away.

As she stared down at the mess on the floor, her immediate reaction was one of immense relief, but then she began to retch uncontrollably. A black cat, which she knew at once must have belonged to the Livingstones, was lying there hideously mutilated; its severed head stared up at her and maggots were crawling out of its eye sockets. Cathy could not trust herself to speak and pressed the button on the locket to receive.

'What's wrong? Hang on, we're on our way.' Harding's voice echoed through the microphone on her chest.

'It's all right. Mark's not here, it's only a dead cat.' Cathy was shaking uncontrollably. 'The house seems to be empty.'

'If you're quite sure that you don't need help, it'll be safer if you walk back then, in case anyone's watching. We'll be waiting for you at the corner.'

'Right, I'll start now.'

Cathy wiped the perspiration from her forehead with her handkerchief and walked quickly towards the door. She had just stepped outside on to the landing, when something hit her a crushing blow on the back of her head and everything went black.

★   ★   ★

Janice could feel the excitement welling up inside her as she waited for the two men in the front bedroom of the house. The moment she had been waiting for ever since she had started to make her plan was near at hand. Although she knew that the woman couldn't possibly get there before midnight, she kept glancing at the luminous dial of her watch, willing the minutes to go by faster.

She was visualizing in her mind's eye exactly what she was going to do to the woman whose father had been responsible for all her misery, when one of the men by her side tugged at the sleeve of her jumper. Looking out of the window, she saw the flash of a torch from the front garden of the house opposite.

'That's the all clear signal; she'll be walking up the road on her own.'

Minutes later, they heard the sound of

a cough from below, then heavy foot-steps on the stairs and saw the wavering light from the torch, which sent shadows dancing though the half-open door. The two men crept out of the door and Janice followed them, waiting at the threshold. Quite distinctly, she heard the woman's gasp of horror, the sound of her retching and then the muffled conversation. Surely, she thought, there can't be two of them. She shrank back when she heard footsteps coming out on to the landing and then came the soft thud as the cosh struck home.

When she went to investigate, she saw that one of the men was supporting the woman under the arms, while the other was standing there, looking in her direction and holding his finger in front of his lips. He tip-toed towards Janice and led her back into the front bedroom.

'She's got a two-way radio round her neck,' he whispered. 'I'm going to disconnect it; hold the torch for me and make as little noise as possible.'

While the second man continued to support the unconscious woman, he eased up her jumper, uncoupled the belt from around her waist and with his pocket knife, cut through every wire he could see. Only then, did he relax.

'Christ, that was close! We'll have to get a move on now; there's no time to contact Mulligan.'

The larger of the two men slung the crumpled figure over his shoulder and hurried down the stair after the one with the torch. They left by the back door, securing both it and the one at the front, and once through the hole in the wall at the end of the back garden, they began to cross the large area of rubble, where the slum clearance was already in progress. Within a few minutes, they were picking their way across some railway lines.

'If you don't want to be incinerated, you'd better look sharp,' hissed the second man to Janice. 'Here, take this other torch.'

As they went over the track, Janice was in a constant state of terror in case she stumbled over the live rail. Even with the unconscious woman over his shoulder, the large man moved quickly and confidently and she had considerable difficulty in keeping up. After what to her seemed an age, they came out on to another dimly lit road through a narrow passage-way. Parked at the exit, there was a car with its engine running and they threw themselves inside.

'All clear George?'

'Haven't seen or heard a thing,' the driver replied and accelerated smoothly away.

'Christ, I hope she's worth it.' The large man was mopping his brow with a filthy handkerchief and was still breathing heavily.

'She'll be worth it all right, just you see.' Janice grinned to herself in anticipation of what was to come.

'Don't you think the warehouse is a bit close?' The man in the front seat turned half round to face them.

'No, everything's set up there and they'd never find us in a month of Sundays. In any case, there's nowhere else we can go. She can also scream to her heart's content there — it's at least half a mile from the nearest house. That's what you want, isn't it?'

'That's what I'm paying for and I won't settle for anything less.'

'I still don't like it.'

'Shut up Fred. You can keep watch outside if you like — George can join in the fun; he hasn't seen any action yet.'

After less than ten minutes, they drew up outside a parking lot full of lorries and they all got out with the exception of Fred.

'You know exactly where we are. If you see or hear anything suspicious, don't hang about, come straight in and we can scarper through the back entrance; there's another car set up behind the parking lot.'

The metal door of the warehouse was on runners and as it slid sideways, it gave a loud series of squeaks. George closed it after them and pressed the switch on the wall. They all blinked uncertainly in the strong light and the large man dropped his burden on to the floor.

'She still seems to be unconsious. You didn't hit her too hard, did you?' Janice asked anxiously.

''Course I didn't; just gave her a little

tap, that's all.' He took hold of Cathy's ear and gave it a vicious twist. 'There, what did I tell you?' he said, as she gave a cry of pain and opened her eyes.

'Good. Stand her up.'

The man forced her arm up behind her back and lifted her to her feet. Janice slowly came forward until she was standing only a foot or two away and then hit her hard across the mouth with the back of her hand and smiled as a trickle of blood began to course its way down the young woman's chin. Janice lifted up her head by pulling on her hair and spat accurately into her eye.

'You've been wondering who I am and why I've taken your precious son, haven't you? Well, I'll tell you; your father had me put away for three years and that's a long time. He lives for you and your little boy, doesn't he? Well, for the rest of his life he's not going to be able to bear to look at either of you. We're going to smash your face up so that no dental or plastic surgeon will be able to do anything about it and then we'll start on your hands. As for your son, he's all right at the moment, but we'll fetch him later and do the same to him in front of you. But first of all, I want to hear you scream and then I'll let the boys have some fun with you before you get all messed up. Right, get her ready.'

The two men ripped Cathy's clothes off and one of them held her upright with her arms behind her back.

'You were right,' said Ron, the large man. 'She's not bad, not bad at all.'

He reached down with his hand and laughed coarsely when Cathy let out a strangled moan.

'Your time will come,' said Janice. 'Now, get out of my way.' She lit a cigarette and drew hard on it until the tip glowed red. 'They tell me you've had a nervous breakdown — it'll be interesting to see what our particular form of 'shock' treatment does for you.'

She took another pull on the cigarette and selecting a spot on the young woman's left breast, pressed it firmly against the skin and held it there until it went out. The girl's back arched as she fought to escape the agonizing pain and her scream reverberated round the warehouse.

'Holy Moses,' said Ron, drawing in his breath with a sharp hiss.

Janice relit the cigarette and laughed as the white-faced girl shook her head from side to side.

'No, oh please no.'

The second time, her scream was even louder and had an unearthly quality to it.

'I think that will have to do for the time being; we don't want her fainting on us, do we?' Janice moved well away to the side so that she could view the whole scene. 'That was only the hors d'oeuvres, you know. Before we continue, we must give Ron his reward; I'm told, my dear Mrs Livingstone, that his tastes are rather unusual.

★   ★   ★

As soon as they reached the end of the road and saw that Cathy was not in sight, Livingstone and Harding knew that something was wrong. While Harding made frantic signals towards the police

186

car, Livingstone sprinted up the road and by the time it had drawn up outside number forty-three, he was already battering at the door. It did not stand the assault of the two powerful men for long and with a final splintering crash, flew open and hung sideways from one hinge. They found the two-way radio almost at once at the top of the stairs.

'They must have taken her out through the back. You see what's out there and I'll organize the men at the front.'

By the time Harding had reached the road, he could hear the sounds of Livingstone's attack on the rear door. Gould was getting out of the car and one look at his face was enough to see that the news was bad.

'We've lost contact with that homing device — the signal began to get weaker as we came up the road.'

'What's out behind the house?'

Gould consulted his map. 'They're clearing this whole area here to build a new housing estate — there's nothing much but a lot of rubble for about half a mile and then there's the railway.'

'That gives them quite a lot of choice then.'

'No, I don't think so. For them to have got out of range so quickly, they must have gone almost directly away from us. I'll send the car with the detector to patrol the area across the railway line at once.'

'It's a pretty forlorn hope isn't it?'

'I'm afraid so.'

The next twenty minutes were the worst that any of them had ever spent. They had found one of Cathy's shoes about twenty yards from the wall behind the house; when he saw it, Harding was terrified lest it was the one containing the homing device, which might have been damaged at the result of its fall and rendered inactive, but the heel was quite solid and he breathed a sigh of relief.

'I'm sure that she must have kicked it off deliberately,' he said with a confidence that he certainly didn't feel and at least it makes it quite certain which way they went.'

They made a thorough search of the house, but apart from the cat, found nothing. Harding was just about to try to give the other two men some words of comfort when he saw the looks on their faces and thought better of it.

'I'm going outside to see if there's any news,' said Gould, after they had been standing around for some minutes in an awkward silence.

The other two men followed him and began to pace up and down uneasily until the Inspector's shout sent them running towards the car.

'Our detector van has made contact with the homing device.' His voice was high pitched with excitement. 'I've told them to wait until we join them — they're only a couple of miles away.'

Before they had time to close the doors, the car was off with a burst of acceleration that left parallel streaks of rubber on the road, they took the corner on two wheels, their blue light flashing, and in a little under five minutes, drew up behind the police car parked under a street light.

'The signal's very strong here, sir. There's a bloke in a car just round the

corner parked in front of some ware-
houses; he's alone and may be keeping
watch — I can't see what else he could be
doing there at this time of night.'

'Let me deal with this,' said Harding.
'If we're wrong, it might save you some
embarrassment.'

Watching from the corner, Livingstone
saw him weaving down the pavement; he
was singing a bawdy song and just short
of the car, hung on to a lamp-post for a
moment and then tottered forwards,
holding the roof of the car for support.

'Gotta light mate?'

The man in the car wound down the
window and Harding's hand shot in and
his knife just pricked the skin over his
Adam's apple.

'One peep out of you son, and you'll be
breathing out of a distinctly unusual
place.'

He signalled with his free hand and the
other two men sprinted up, wrenched
open the rear doors and got in.

'Are you sure about this?' Livingstone
said in a hoarse whisper.

'Take a look down there.' Harding

made a gesture with his thumb. 'That's Cathy's other shoe if I'm not much mistaken. Look after this bloke for a moment will you Jim while I get in the front?'

'No you don't.'

The detective put a neck lock on the driver as he stretched out his hand to press the horn button and tightened his grip until the man began to drum on the floor with his heels.

'Now sonny Jim,' said Harding when he had got in beside him, 'you're going to tell me exactly where they are and what they're doing, otherwise I'll start on some surgery.'

As the man began to speak, Gould could feel Livingstone tensing up beside him and he put a restraining hand on his shoulder as his hand went towards the handle on the car door.

'I know exactly how you feel, but we'll have to take it quietly; if they hear us coming, they might kill her and the baby too. We'll have to surround the place, there's probably a back entrance.'

At that moment, they all heard the terrible scream.

'Forget it,' Gould shouted. 'Let's go.'

It was the work of a few seconds to gag the driver and Harding frog-marched him up the road to the waiting police car. He had only just got back when the second scream rang out and the three of them ran across the open ground towards the entrance to the warehouse, pausing momentarily outside the sliding door. Harding gave it a tentative push and cursed softly when it gave a squeak.

'This bloody thing's bound to make a hell of a din when we shift it properly,' he whispered.

'At least it's not locked,' said Livingstone.

'No, thank God. I can see light shining through the gap here, it must be the right place. Let's all shove together and then rush them.'

Livingstone was to remember that scene for the rest of his life. The naked girl with the two large red patches disfiguring her white body was being held by one man while the other was kneeling in front of her. He just had time to turn round before Livingstone, letting out a roar like an enraged bull, charged across the warehouse floor and hit him a terrible blow in the face. He felt the bones crunch under his fist and then, big though the man was, lifted him up as though he were a child, raised him high above his head and hurled him towards a pile of packing cases. The wood splintered and the man's coarse cry was cut off as he lay there, twitching and moaning feebly.

Livingstone lifted his foot and, taking careful aim, kicked him with a force that jarred his leg right up to the hip. The man's back arched like a bow and an unearthly howl came from his lips, then he jerked convulsively for a few moments and lay still. When Livingstone turned round, Harding was holding the other man round the neck with a grip of iron and Gould, having draped his raincoat over Cathy's back, was supporting her under her arms.

He gently wiped her swollen mouth with his handkerchief. 'It's all right now, it's all over.'

'Don't worry about me,' she whispered hoarsely, 'I'm O.K.. Get that woman

— she can't have gone far.'

While Gould was handcuffing the two men and Livingstone looked after Cathy, Harding started to search the warehouse. He soon found the rear exit and before long the place was swarming with police.

Livingstone lifted Cathy up in his arms and gently began to rock her back and forth.

'Who is she?'

'Some mad-woman your father-in-law sentenced.'

'Was she the one who burned you?'

Cathy nodded and he saw her eyes fill with tears and then she began to sob uncontrollably.

'There, there,' he said softly, 'you're quite safe now.'

'But Mark isn't — they've still got him and that woman's escaped, I know she has.'

Livingstone was as doubtful as any of them when Cathy begged him to take her back to Chelsea after she had had her head X-rayed and her burns dressed at St Gregory's Hospital, but after what she had been through on his behalf, he would have agreed to anything she asked.

When Mrs Trapnell had tucked her up in the bedroom on the top floor and she had been given a sedative, he sat holding her hand until she had gone off to sleep. He looked down at the girl lying there peacefully.

'If only you knew,' he said, half to himself, 'and if only I could have helped you more.'

He relived their afternoon by the Thames and spoke to her in a way that he never could have done if she had been awake. He had never really understood the value of the psychiatrist's couch before and indeed almost despised that type of introversion, which he had always looked on as self-indulgence, but when he had finished, he felt a calm he had not experienced for months. He sat there for another ten minutes, then gently disengaged his hand, just brushed her fingers with his lips and tip-toed out of the room.

# 8

Mulligan, crouching behind the hedge in the garden of the house opposite number forty-three, gave a grunt of satisfaction when he saw the young woman turn the corner and start to walk up the road. He waited until she was only fifty yards away, and when he was as sure as he could be that she wasn't being followed, gave three short flashes with his torch. Almost at once there was an acknowledgement from the room on the first floor of the house across the road and when she had disappeared through the front door, he cocked his ear expectantly.

He did not have to wait long and smiled grimly to himself when the sound of the woman retching came through clearly to him — it all seemed to be going more smoothly than he had anticipated. He glanced at his watch and was about to get to his feet to ease his cramped muscles, when he heard the sound of running feet and the roar of a car being driven fast in low gear.

Mulligan stretched himself out flat on the ground, knowing at once that the police had set a trap after all. Many of the boards in the low fence below the hedge were broken and rotting and he was able to see quite clearly what was going on. He heard them battering away at the rear door and calculated that Ron and the others would have had at best only five minutes start. It was just as well, he thought, that he had selected the place so carefully — they stood an excellent chance of getting away across the railway — but it would be just like that bone-head Ron to stick to the warehouse. Although there wasn't all that much risk of the police finding it, it was still much too close for comfort.

Mulligan heard them pacing up and down and pressed his face into the earth, his heart pounding wildly, when they came by within two or three feet of him; one of them only had to glance over the top of the hedge and they would be bound to see him. His worst fears about the operation were realized when he heard them talking about the detector and as soon as they had driven away, he ran up the path and through the open door of the house behind him. He had only just pulled it to, when the road was lit up by the powerful headlights and through the letter-box, he saw two uniformed policemen, both with Alsatians on leads, go into number forty-three.

Mulligan had once been captured by one of those tracker dogs. He had only been sixteen at the time and had snatched a handbag at a greyhound race meeting; he was running away when the dark shape had launched itself at him, knocking him down and worrying his arm, all the time growling menacingly. He had never forgotten that experience and ever since had had a profound fear of large dogs. He decided not to hang about any longer, running out through the back of the house over some waste ground and not slackening pace until he reached his car parked half a mile away.

Mulligan knew the area around the warehouse like the back of his hand — he ought to have done, he had been brought up there and his father still ran a haulage business from a lot across the road and that had been the main reason for selecting it. He climbed over the fence which enclosed the lorry park and shinned up the metal fire-escape ladder set into the brick-work of the office block.

From the flat roof of the building, he had a grandstand view of the front of the warehouse. The whole area was swarming with police and within minutes, he saw the girl being carried out, then helped into one of the police cars and driven off. It was another hour before all was quiet again and he felt it was safe enough to climb down and let himself in through the back door. He picked up the phone in the office and dialled a number.

'Grey here.'

'It's Mulligan, boss. The whole thing's gone wrong; the police set a trap and they've pinched all three of our men.'

'What about the woman?'

'I think she must have got away. I was watching the whole time and there was no sign of her.'

'I see.'

There was a very long pause.

'Are you still there, boss?'

'Yes. Be quiet will you, I'm trying to think. No, on second thoughts, give me your number and I'll ring you back in five minutes.' Grey was as good as his word. 'Get round to the 'Twilight Club',' he said when he came back on the line, 'pick up Rita Channing and bring her here. I also want the contents of the safe . . . And Mulligan.'

'Yes, boss.'

'You'd better hurry if you want to get there before the police. And one last thing — don't tell anyone where you're taking her; I'll leave it to you to make up a suitable story. Is that all quite clear?'

'Yes, boss.'

When Grey rang off, he had a thoughtful frown on his face; Mulligan was reliable enough, but not exactly quick on the uptake — that's why he made such a good second in command. If he made a mess of this, so much the worse; it would be a pity not to have dealt with that wretched woman, who in the end had caused him so much trouble, but he had no intention of taking it on himself. He stretched out an arm for the telephone.

'Dwyer? Grey here. As I thought, it's blown up on me. Can you get to the field by five? . . . Good, I'll be waiting there.'

★　★　★

All was quiet when Mulligan arrived at the 'Twilight Club.'

'Where's Rick?'

'In his office. Do you want me to get him?'

'No, that's all right.'

The barman went off with a smirk on his lips and Mulligan stood there for a moment, looking down at the tables clustered round the tiny dance floor. Rita was sitting with a middle-aged man, who, at that moment, leaned across and whispered something in her ear. He saw her shake her head and move away slightly. It was the current gimmick at the club to dress the girls in see-through white blouses and very short skirts and as he watched, the man put one hand on her knee and with the other poured her out another drink. Mulligan shook his head and went off up the stairs — he had a profound contempt for the suckers who came to places like this.

He paused at the office door, listened for a moment and then inserted his key into the lock, twisted it and flung the door open. No wonder the barman had been grinning, he thought as he surveyed the scene.

'All right Angela, leave us will you?'

The girl slid off the desk, hastily scooped her clothes off the floor and made a dash for the door. Mulligan put an arm across the entrance and pulled her up short.

'Take over from Rita will you and tell her I want to see her up here right away?'

The girl shot out like a frightened rabbit and Mulligan turned towards the other man, who was trying frantically to put his trousers back on.

'You won't . . . '

'Relax, Rick. I've just come to warn you that the boss has had a tip-off that the club is going to be raided tonight. He wants Rita out of the way as she's been inside so recently and for you to make sure that the place is clean. See to it will you?'

'Yes, Mr Mulligan.'

Mulligan enjoyed the mister, even though he knew that it was Grey, not him, who produced this effect on people.

'And don't do it again on the premises — you know the boss won't have it. Now, give me the keys to the safe, will you?'

When Rick had gone, he opened the safe and drew his breath in sharply when he saw how much money there was there — the gambling rooms must have been doing better than he had realized. Inside the safe, there was a large canvas bag, half full of small change, and he emptied it out, filling it up with the bundles of notes. He had just locked up again, when he heard a tentative knock on the door.

'Come in . . . Ah, Rita, Mr Grey would like to see you at his house and asked me to collect you.'

'What about?'

Mulligan could see at once how

nervous she was and did his best to put her at her ease.

'I don't know, but he seemed to be in a very good mood. You have worked hard and I know he's pleased with you; he's been talking for some time about opening a new club in Sardinia and it may be something to do with that.'

There had been rumours about Grey's new venture for some time, but it was obvious that the girl was not entirely reassured.

'But why at this time of night?'

'Didn't Rick tell you? The boss had a tip-off about a possible police raid tonight and he didn't want you to get involved — you've only been out for about six months, haven't you?'

'Yes, that's right.'

All the way to the country house in Hertfordshire, Rita sat hunched up on the back seat of the large car. She was perfectly well aware of the occupational risks of being a hostess and although Mulligan had never tried any funny business with her, or with any of the other girls for that matter, and she knew that he was very close to Grey, she nevertheless had the feeling that something odd was going on.

She was somewhat reassured when Grey came out to the drive to meet them, smiling warmly. He was wearing a dinner jacket and smoking a cigar and looked so immaculate that she was acutely conscious of how cheap she must look in her shoddy, titillating costume, particularly after he had taken her coat when they went into the hall.

'I was just telling Rita about the police raid on the club,' said Mulligan.

'Quite so. Come in here, my dear.'

Rita had never seen such opulence in her life; the furnishings alone must have cost several thousand and she hadn't known that carpets with such thick pile existed. They went straight through the room and she was ushered into a book-lined study.

'Would you mind waiting in here for a few moments? I won't keep you long.'

Grey turned the key quietly in the lock and poured Mulligan a glass of whisky from the sideboard.

'Tell me exactly what happened.'

He listened in silence while the other man gave him a detailed account of all that he had seen from the top of the office block.

'You say that both Ron and George were brought out on stretchers?' Mulligan nodded. 'What about the Livingstone woman?'

'She was carried out by her husband, but she obviously wasn't in very bad shape — she was able to get into the car on her own.'

'Pity.' Grey drew hard on his cigar and slowly let the smoke filter out of his mouth. 'You know Mulligan, we're going to have to assume that those men will talk.'

'I shouldn't worry about that, boss; they know perfectly well that they have more to fear from you than the police.'

'I wasn't thinking about the police. You know about that trouble with Bruce the other night at the casino?' Mulligan nodded again. 'Well, the man who took him away with Mrs Livingstone and another bloke is called Harding and I've since discovered that he works for the special security services; I know those men — they can be very rough indeed. Ron is tough enough, but somehow I think George will crack.'

'What are we going to do?'

'We're going to have to get out and lie low for a while and what's more, tonight. But first of all I want you to deal with that woman that Rita brought along. She's managed to wreck everything we've worked so hard to set up for the last five years and I want her eliminated.'

'But how am I going to find her, boss?'

'Why do you think I went to all the trouble of bringing Rita Channing here? She'll know where she's likely to be hiding out if anyone does. Now, this is what I propose . . . '

⋆   ⋆   ⋆

At first, Rita just wandered around the study, looking at the books, but none of them interested her particularly, and when after ten minutes, the two men had not reappeared, she began to get even more nervous and went across to the door. Panic began to well up inside her when not only did she find it locked, but on looking round she saw something that she had not noticed before — the room had no windows. By the time Grey did come back, she was feeling sick with fear.

'Sorry to have kept you for so long.'

The girl swallowed painfully. 'Why did you lock me in? What do you want with me?'

'Sit down and I'll tell you.' He waved an arm towards the studio couch and Rita sank down as if hypnotized, her hands shaking uncontrollably. 'I want the real name and address of that woman you introduced to me and anything else you know about her.'

'I don't know anything about her, you see she . . . '

Grey held up his hand. 'I think you do know all right, and before I ask you again, listen for a moment. That woman has caused me to lose three good men, the police are bound to start taking an interest in the business that I have taken years to build up and I propose to deal with her. If you don't tell me about it, I assure you you'll regret it bitterly. By the way, did I tell you that this room is sound proof? Well, I'm waiting.'

'I don't know anything about her — I swear it.' Rita licked her lips and looked around wildly.

'As you wish.' He nodded to Mulligan, who was standing directly behind her. 'Tie her down.'

Rita Channing hardly put up a struggle. She seemed half paralysed with fear and a few moments later, she was stretched out on the couch, pinned down by two broad leather straps, one of which went across her shins and the other across her forearms, which were stretched down by her side.

Grey drew up a stool, picked up a pair of pliers and opened and closed them a few times.

'Well?'

Rita shook her head frantically as Grey carefully took her right thumb nail between the jaws of the pliers and when he gripped it tightly and started to pull, she began to scream and then fainted away.

'Interesting that,' said Grey, getting to his feet. 'She showed more courage than I would have credited — although I suppose it's always possible that she really doesn't know.'

'Do you want me to bring her round, boss?'

'All in good time, Mulligan. As I told you outside, I had no intention of marking her in any way — that little charade was just to soften her up a bit.' He went across to the desk and picked up a large syringe full of a pale yellow liquid. He held it up to the light and expelled the last few bubbles of air. 'Pentothal — it's often called the 'truth drug'; it isn't, of course, but it does sometimes have a way of loosening reluctant tongues. Now, I'm going to insert the needle into this vein on the back of her hand and I want you to inject about this amount each time I nod my head; I particularly don't want her to see what we're doing.'

Rita recovered consciousness to the feel of her forehead being gently sponged with a damp flannel. She struggled to get up and when she felt the restraint of the leather straps, she quite suddenly remembered where she was and what had happened. She opened her mouth to scream, but as she did so, began to experience a delightful, soporific feeling, which gradually stole over her.

The soft voice, which gently asked her questions, seemed devoid of all menace. Why shouldn't she tell him about her time in prison and her friendship with Janice Beaton? The man seemed so kind and understanding and what possible harm could come from it? Janice had seemed so pleased about her new flat, too.

Grey snapped shut his note-book and got to his feet. 'Right, give her all that's remaining in the syringe.'

The girl, who had been muttering to herself, went silent and her head fell to one side.

'I think there's an excellent chance that you'll find this woman Janice Beaton at her flat. As she's only just got out of prison, it's most likely that she's got nowhere else to go. See to it now, will you?'

'What about Rita, boss?'

'Ah yes, Rita.' He looked down at the girl for a long time and then smiled. 'Give me that other syringe will you?'

When he had injected the entire contents, he removed the needle and then spoke quietly to Mulligan for a full five minutes.

'I'll wait here until you get back. If you bring it off satisfactorily, there'll be ten thousand in it for you.'

'Suppose the woman isn't there?'

'Wait in her flat until six o'clock and if she hasn't shown up by then, just carry out the first part of our plan.'

Grey stood on the steps in front of the house and shook his head slowly as he watched Mulligan drive away. The man had handed over the money from the 'Twilight Club' without a word — such honesty was deeply touching. It was just as well too, that he was so thick; the poor fool had really believed that he would be waiting for him with the money on his return.

Grey glanced at his watch and walked briskly back into the house; time was getting on and it wouldn't do to be late at the field. He hurried up the stairs, collected the two large suitcases from the landing and minutes later, was on the road. He had known for years that the time would come when he would have to clear out and his plans had been carefully laid. Dwyer would fly him to Ireland, he would take a long holiday and with the capital he had been steadily accumulating over the preceding ten years, there were all sorts of interesting possibilities for the future.

★　★　★

When Janice moved to the side of the young woman in the warehouse, she felt a throb of excitement deep inside her. The man was monstrously big and there was no doubt about it, the humiliation and the mental and physical destruction would be complete.

As Ron approached the girl, she heard a slight squeak that came from the direction of the warehouse door. She acted instinctively, without conscious thought, and ducked down out of sight.

The heavy packing cases were stacked up in great piles, several layers thick, and by the time the police had forced their way in, Janice had squeezed between them, closing the gaps behind her as she penetrated more deeply. After the initial uproar, the relative silence that followed was almost as unnerving and Janice lay absolutely still as the sound of foot-steps came nearer.

'She must have gone this way — there's a door at the back here.'

Heavy boots grated on the concrete floor and Janice blessed her decision not to have tried to get away. She had not run any distance for years, had no idea of the lie of the land behind the warehouse and it was obvious that they would have caught her in no time at all.

Ten minutes later, she heard the main door being pulled across and was just wondering how long it would be wise to wait, when George's voice came through clearly to her, high-pitched with fear.

'You can't do anything to me.'

'Whatever gave you that idea? Let's get this straight, my friend, I'm nothing to do with the police, they've gone away, and so you can forget about rules and rights — you have none. You're going to tell me all you know, otherwise I'll start to work on you in a way that'll make what you did to that girl look like gentle massage. I might tell you, I'm an expert.'

'I had nothing to do with it, I swear to you . . . '

'I'm crying my eyes out. Well? . . . You don't believe me? You think I'm bluffing?'

He began to tell him in lingering detail exactly what he was going to do to him and as the man's relentless voice went on, George began to blubber and then gave one high-pitched scream of agony.

'That was just a sample. Ready to talk?'

George held out for a moment or two longer, but then there was no stopping him. When he had finished, Janice knew that it wouldn't be long before the police discovered her flat; they knew about Grey and worst of all, they knew about Rita, who was the one person apart from Sandra, who was aware of her address. She cursed herself for having told her friend about it, but then put it out of her mind and concentrated on what she had to do next.

She was no longer worried about Grey, he had had it; even if the police didn't get him, he would be far too busy to be concerned about her. The first thing she had to do was to get out of this place safely and then she would decide what to do about the Livingstones. She hadn't finished with them, not by a long chalk, and she still had her trump card, the baby, who with any luck would remain safely hidden for some time yet.

After everyone had left the warehouse, Janice forced herself to wait for an hour and then took her shoes off and felt her way in the dark to the sliding door at the front of the warehouse. She tried to ease it open and when it failed to move, pushed with all her strength on one of the metal struts. When this produced no result either, she raised her fist to pound it with frustration, but then froze in horror when she heard the cough from outside, shortly followed by the sound of someone blowing their nose.

Janice very nearly lost her head completely — it had somehow never occurred to her that the police would secure the warehouse and put a guard on it. If they had done the same with the door at the rear of the building, she was lost — she had already seen that there were no windows. She began to hope again when she found that it was unlocked, merely bolted from the inside.

It took her a good five minutes to shoot each bolt back. They were both rusty and tight fitting and every time she lost patience and tried to hurry things up, they let out piercing squeaks that set her heart pounding. At last, they were fully drawn back and she took her gun out of her handbag, pulling the door open carefully and listening for several minutes before she dared to venture outside.

Janice was a nervous wreck by the time she reached the main road. Every shadow seemed to hide a policeman and at each moment, she expected a torch to be shone at her and a heavy hand to be placed on her shoulder. Once she tripped over a piece of tubular scaffolding lying

217

on the ground and a cat, which had been sitting on a nearby wall, fled, shrieking in terror. Janice couldn't stand it any longer; she threw caution to the winds and ran until she was near to collapse.

She was leaning against a lamp-post, fighting to regain her breath, when she saw the headlights of an approaching car and was so exhausted that she couldn't raise the energy to move, even when she realized that it was slowing down.

'What's up then?'

The girl in the passenger seat had wound down the window and was leaning out. Janice breathed a sigh of relief when she saw that the couple were alone in the car and limped across the pavement towards them. There was no doubt that she looked a terrible mess; her hair was all over the place, her face was streaked with dirt and her tights were torn in several places.

'Two men gave me a lift back from this club; they took me to a warehouse and they . . . they . . . ' She began to sob quietly.

'Come on Carole, let's go.'

'But we can't leave her like this.'

The young man glanced anxiously over his shoulder. 'I don't like the look of this place.'

'Don't be such a coward. If you won't help her, I will.' the girl opened the door and got out. 'Come on, get in the back with me. Do you want us to take you to the police?'

'I just want to go home.'

'Where do you live?'

Janice told her and had no need to hide her relief when, after grumbling for a bit, the young man agreed to drive her to her flat. She took her time when the couple had disappeared round the corner in their car; twenty minutes sitting in the back of it had given her time to calm down. She didn't think the police would have had time to discover her address, but she wasn't going to take unnecessary chances.

She made a complete circuit of the block, and only when she had satisfied herself that there was no movement from any of the windows in her flat and there were no suspicious cars in the neighbourhood, did she go into the lobby.

Janice went up in the lift to the floor above and then walked down the stairs, waiting for several minutes before approaching her front door. She opened the letter-box, listened carefully and when she heard nothing, let herself in and switched on the light in the hall.

If she hadn't been quite so keyed up, Janice probably wouldn't have noticed it, but directly she looked round, she knew that something was wrong. At first, she couldn't put her finger on it, but then she remembered; earlier that evening, she had decided not to take her gun with her, but on the way out had changed her mind and had gone back into the bedroom to fetch it. She was absolutely certain that she had shut the door after her, and now it was half open.

Janice took the gun out of her handbag, slipped off the safety catch and tip-toed across the hall. When she looked through the crack where the hinges were, there was enough light for her to see that a figure was stretched out on the bed. She transferred the pistol to her left hand, flicked down the switch and threw open the door.

Rita was lying on the bed stark naked; her head had been propped up on the pillows and her sightless eyes were staring at her. Janice drew in her breath with a sharp hiss and recoiled in horror, her back to the wall.

'I thought you were never coming.' Mulligan was sitting in the chair by the dressing table with his legs crossed and an automatic, with a long silencer attached to its barrel, resting on one knee. 'Mr Grey is very annoyed with you — you have caused him a great deal of trouble one way and another.'

Janice licked her dry lips. 'What do you want?'

'I don't want anything. I'm going to shoot you and leave the gun with Rita's fingerprints on it — you should have realized that it doesn't pay to annoy Mr Grey. It'll give the police something to think about, particularly if both of you are found naked, but I don't suppose they'll be all that surprised if half of what I heard this evening about your behaviour in

221

prison is true. Pity about Rita — shooting you was obviously too much for the poor girl's conscience and she committed suicide.'

'The police will know at once that she's been murdered.'

'Do you really think that Mr Grey wouldn't have thought about a detail like that? They'll find her blood full of barbiturates and you'll see that I've taken the precaution of leaving an empty bottle of butobarbitone on the bed-side table.'

'Also with her finger-prints on it?'

Mulligan looked sharply across at the woman who was still standing against the wall facing him sideways, as she had been ever since she had whirled round at the sound of his voice. He had a nagging suspicion that something was wrong; she was far too cool and confident. He took a firmer grip on his gun and raised the barrel slightly.

'Naturally.'

Janice was absolutely certain that Mulligan hadn't seen her revolver, but his movement had not escaped her and she knew that she only had seconds in which to distract him. She turned towards him a fraction more.

'There's a good deal of money hidden in this flat — we could share it. I know what you're thinking; you could kill me and take all of it, but you'd never find it before the police get here.'

She glanced towards the wardrobe and Mulligan grinned as he followed her gaze.

'You shouldn't have done that, it makes it . . . '

He did see her move, but far too late and the bullet hit him in the chest, slamming him against the back of the chair. His own gun fell on to the carpet with a dull thud and the man looked down stupidly at the stain which was rapidly discolouring his white shirt. Mulligan half rose to his feet, his finger clasped to his chest and took one hesitant step, then fell forwards and lay still, a thin trickle of blood dribbling from his mouth.

For a moment, Janice stood there motionless. The noise of the gun going off had sounded like a thunderclap to her, but after she had opened the front door and listened for several minutes, she was satisfied that no one had been disturbed. Rather than being upset by what had happened, she felt a new surge of confidence at having dealt with Mulligan so efficiently. She had never seen a man killed before, let alone done it herself, and she felt an overwhelming sense of power. Who the hell did Grey think he was?

She took the money in the suitcase from the wardrobe, quickly packed a few things in a hold-all, then went into the sitting room and lay back on the sofa. Fifteen minutes later, she had worked out a plan — for it to be successful, she was going to need a bit of luck, but she reckoned she should get away with it.

Janice was just about to leave, when she decided that perhaps Mulligan's idea hadn't been such a bad one after all. She wiped her gun carefully all over with a clean handkerchief, pressed Rita's hand around it and than placed it on the bedside table next to the empty pill-bottle. Finally, she put the dead girl under the bedclothes, tucked her in neatly and picked Mulligan's revolver off the floor, unscrewing the silencer and putting it into her handbag. As the man had said, that should give the police food for thought. Before she left, she took one last look at the dead man, reliving the excitement of the moment when she had shot him.

# 9

'How is she?'

'She was still asleep when I last had a look.'

Livingstone showed Gould into the living room and poured him out a cup of coffee.

'She really ought to be in hospital after having had a bang on the head like that.'

'I know, but she was so determined to come back here and see it through that I talked the doctor into agreeing to let her do what she wanted. I thought it would be better for her in the long run.'

Gould nodded his agreement. 'I think you were quite right.'

'So do I.'

The two men whirled round. 'Cathy!' said Gould. 'What on earth do you think you're doing?'

'I'm all right thanks.'

'You don't look it, I must say — you're as white as a sheet.'

'Just a bit wobbly, that's all. Did that woman get away?'

'I'm afraid so, but I was just about to tell John that at least we've found out who she is.'

'How did you work that miracle?'

'It wasn't all that difficult as it turned out; David Harding managed to get one of those men to talk, don't ask me how. Their boss is a man called Grey, who runs a string of clubs, and that woman employed him to lay on the ransom demand and the rest. The two of them had originally made contact through one of his hostesses, a girl called Rita Channing. This morning, a window cleaner, who was working on a block of flats in Kensington, saw two bodies in a room of an apartment on the third floor. One of them was this woman Rita — we were able to identify her from her prints; she was only let out of Holloway six months ago and the flat was also covered with the prints of one Janice Beaton, who had been inside at the same time.'

'Not the call-girl case woman?'

'Correct in one and of course she was

sentenced by your father-in-law, John.'

'Who was the second person in the flat?'

'A man whom we haven't been able to identify yet. We also found some baby's clothes and I was wondering, John, if you would go round there with me to identify them.'

'All right, but what about Mark?'

'I was just coming to that. A search of the flat makes it absolutely certain that he's not been kept there and as, according to that bloke Harding questioned, Janice Beaton had been with them almost continuously in the last few days, it looks as if she arranged for him to be looked after somewhere quite different.' He didn't say that he thought it more than likely that the little boy was dead already. 'I would suggest that we put out his photo in the papers tomorrow morning and on TV — someone might recognize him. I don't see much point in publishing his name just yet. What do you think?'

Livingstone got up and paced around for a minute or two. 'I agree,' he said finally. 'It's going to mean making certain that Mary has no contact with the media, but that shouldn't be too difficult. Are you sure you'll be all right here on your own Cathy?'

'Quite, thanks. I'll just be ready to answer the phone.'

'O.K. I won't be long.'

She went down to the front door to see them off and as she waved to them, realized with a sense of shock just how close she and John Livingstone had become. He had kissed her good-bye as if it had been the most natural thing in the world and she had not even taken in the fact that he had done it, until the two men were in the car. She blushed as she thought how glad she was that Jim Gould didn't appear to have noticed.

⋆　⋆　⋆

Janice found a parking place within sight of the Livingstones' house soon after eight o'clock and settled down to wait. Earlier, she had walked into an hotel, and had a bath and breakfast and then left without paying, the successful deception

229

doing wonders for her morale.

A constable was on duty outside as usual, but apart from the housekeeper's husband going off to work, nothing further happened until the police car drove up. When she saw the two men leave the house and Mrs Livingstone came to the door, she had a sudden idea, which she decided to put into effect as soon as she saw the housekeeper come out of the basement with a shopping basket.

She drove her car round the corner and then walked briskly up to the Livingstones' front door and rang the bell.

'Ah, good morning officer. I haven't seen you before, I'm Mrs Livingstone's sister. Nice morning, isn't it?'.

The man smiled. 'Makes my job a lot more pleasant, I can tell you.'

'I can imagine.'

As soon as the door started to open, Janice gave it a push and stepped inside.

'Good morning, my dear,' she said loudly, the pistol with its sinister looking silencer pointing straight at the woman in the dressing gown. She kicked the door to behind her and lifted the barrel slightly. 'I've already shot one man dead this morning and it would give me a great deal of pleasure to repeat the dose. Now, get up those stairs.'

Cathy obeyed as if she was in a dream. The woman behind her never gave her a chance; she didn't come any closer than five or six feet and the one time Cathy made a sudden movement while she was dressing, the gun coughed sharply and the bullet slammed into the wall, gouging out a piece of plaster.

'Now listen,' she said when Cathy had finished, we're going out of the front door and down the side street to the left where my car is parked — it's a red Ford. I will tell the constable that we're going for a walk — he thinks I'm your sister. The car is unlocked and you will get into the driving seat. If you try anything on, I'll shoot both you and that flat-foot outside.'

She gave Cathy a vicious prod in the ribs with the gun and they went downstairs side by side. As they left the house, never once did the firm pressure from the silencer at the end of the barrel let up and although Cathy did try to catch the policeman's eye, he merely smiled and saluted and the moment was past.

All the way out of London, Janice never once relaxed her vigilance, keeping the gun only inches from the back of Cathy's neck, but once they were on the open road, she relaxed a bit and settled herself more comfortably on the back seat. At first, Cathy found it a relief that Janice had said nothing apart from giving directions, but after nearly two hours, she could stand it no longer.

'Where are we going?'

'Just to see the baby and complete the business we started last night.'

'What are you going to do to me?'

'Getting a bit worked up are you?' I was wondering how long it would be before you sat up and took notice. Patience, patience, you will soon find out, but I can assure you that whatever else it is, it's not going to be a very pleasant experience. I would have preferred the Judge's daughter to have been here, but one can't have everything.'

'What do you mean?'

'I'm not a complete fool, you know, and I've had my suspicions about you for some time. People who are recovering from nervous breakdowns don't behave in the way that you have and then, you will remember, I was able to have a close look at you last night; I will say this for you, you're not bad looking and you most certainly never had a baby a year ago. Who are you, as a matter of interest?'

'I'm a police officer and we know all about you, Janice Beaton.'

'I'm shaking with fear. If there's one group of people I hate as much as judges, it's screws. I've got enough money in the back of the car to go anywhere I please and when I've finished with you and the baby, I'll enjoy reading about it in the papers. You've been having a ball in that house, haven't you? Disgusting I call it; I saw that Livingstone bloke kiss you when he left this morning — quite touching it was — but he won't be wanting to do it again by the time I've finished with you, oh dear me no.'

In an effort to shut her mind to what

Janice was saying, Cathy looked at the surrounding countryside and suddenly realized where they were. She had once been to watch a water skiing competition at an old water-filled quarry nearby and she suddenly had the germ of an idea; the place she had in mind couldn't be more than a mile away.

Cathy blessed the fact that, purely as a reflex action, she fastened her seat belt on getting into the car, and at least that would give her a chance, slim though it was, something she most certainly would not have if Janice continued to control the situation. The one snag was that the road was practically empty. The only car in sight was an aged Morris Minor just ahead, which was being driven at a snail's pace by an elderly woman. It wasn't much, but better than nothing, and she pulled out to pass, at the same time reaching down to tighten the safety belt as much as possible.

'What are you doing?'

'I can't get comfortable — my chest's still very sore.'

Cathy caught a glimpse of the water on

her left and two hundred yards ahead, saw the break in the trees that she had been hoping for. As quickly as she could, she wound up the window by her side.

'Leave that alone.'

Cathy turned round. 'It's just a bit draughty, that's all.'

Now that her mind was made up, she felt almost cheerful, although her heart was thumping painfully in her chest. She faced the road again and steered straight for the gap to their side. In the rear-view mirror, she saw Janice's eyes widen with horror as the car started to swerve off the road.

'Look out!' she screamed.

It seemed to Cathy as if what occurred next was happening in slow motion. The car shot over the narrow grass verge, was suspended for a moment in mid-air, and then hit the water travelling at fifty miles per hour. In the same moment that the windscreen went opaque, she felt a searing pain across her chest as the seat belt dug into her and then something hit her a stunning blow on the forehead.

★　★　★

Daphne Young settled herself more comfortably behind the wheel of her Morris Minor when she saw the sign indicating a duel carriage-way ahead. Her reflexes were not so quick as they had been, she was more accustomed to going along country lanes and she hated the cut and thrust of driving in London. In fact, she hated the metropolis altogether and would never have dreamt of coming up by car if it hadn't been for the threatened rail strike. Still, her visit had been well worthwhile; tucked away in the country, there was a danger of becoming fossilized and at her age, it was nice to feel that she could still be useful to others. She had found looking after Fiona's children exhausting, but she had coped and a bit of old-fashioned discipline for a change had done them no harm at all.

The traffic had thinned out and once the bright red Ford, which had been following her for a mile or two, had gone by, she relaxed and began to enjoy the scenery, which was particularly attractive at that point; the sun was shining through the trees and she could just make out the glint of water to her left.

Daphne Young glanced back at the road and could not believe her eyes. She blinked and looked again, thinking that it might just be a trick of the light, but there was no doubt about it, the red car had completely disappeared. At that point, the road was quite straight for at least a mile and there had not been time for it to have gone far enough to get out of sight. For an instant, she even wondered if she could have dropped off to sleep for a moment, but she knew perfectly well that she hadn't and in any case, a few seconds later, her worst fears were realized when she saw the tyre marks on the earth and the gaping hole in the hedge where the car had gone through.

The Ford was rocking gently on the surface of the water and through its side window, she was able to make out the woman slumped over the wheel and another figure draped over the back of the front passenger seat. The elderly woman felt sick with agitation and worry — she hadn't swum for twenty years and even if she had been able to reach the car, knew that she wouldn't have been able to do anything. She ran back to the road and waved frantically at the car which was approaching, but the driver swept by without slowing.

Nearly ten minutes went by before Daphne Young was able to get help. Two more cars had gone by without stopping and she was unable to reach the other lane of the dual carriage-way, which at that point was separated from her by nearly fifty yards of dense undergrowth. Finally, in desperation, she stood in the middle of the road, semaphoring with her arms, when she saw a heavy lorry coming into view. She almost cried with relief when it slowed to a halt at the side of the road behind her own car.

'A car had gone off the road into the lake — there are two women trapped inside.'

The lorry driver, a burly man in shirt sleeves and jeans, jumped out of the cab and ran to the edge of the lake. He took one look at the Ford, which was now more than half submerged and began to kick off his shoes. At that moment, the bonnet of the car suddenly dipped forwards and quite slowly the vehicle disappeared beneath the surface, a stream of bubbles being the only sign that anything had been there.

The man went into the water in a flat dive and struck out for the place where the car had submerged. It was only too obvious to her that the man was no swimmer — he made painfully slow progress with his great floundering strokes and by the time he had reached the spot, he was desperately out of breath.

'Was it about here?' he shouted.

'A bit further to your right.'

The man made several attempts to get down to the car, but it was absolutely hopeless. Not only had the bottom of the lake been stirred up, which made it impossible for him to see, but the water was much deeper than he had expected and he lacked the skill to get down far enough. He went on trying for fully five minutes, but then slowly returned to the bank; by this time he was utterly exhausted and had to be helped out of the water by another man who had also stopped.

★   ★   ★

Cathy was in the middle of a confused dream. Janice Beaton had tied her to a chair in a small room and was watching her through the glass spyhole in the door. The woman was laughing at her and pointing at something behind the chair. Cathy turned to look and saw the water pouring from a pipe set into the wall near the floor.

The level took a long time to rise, but this increased the terror as inch by inch the water crept up, covering first her shoes and then climbing inexorably higher. It seemed to hesitate for a moment when it reached the seat, then the dampness engulfed the backs of her thighs and she cried out in pain as it reached the burns on her chest.

Cathy's eyes snapped open and the nightmare faded, but the reality was far worse. She shook her head, trying to pull her fuddled senses together and gradually it all came back to her. Although she knew that she ought to be doing something about getting out, she somehow lacked the will and her mind began to wander.

Quite suddenly, the bonnet of the car dipped and fine sprays of water began to come through the minute cracks in the windscreen, where the glass had gone to sugar. One of them hit her on the forehead and this time she came to properly. If she had been more alert, Cathy might have been able to get out of one of the windows because the water level was still only up to her chest, but in fact she had only just undone her safety belt, when the nose of the car dipped even more sharply and quite slowly, the whole vehicle sank beneath the surface.

The downward tilt increased so much that Cathy was thrown towards the steering wheel, but then the front of the car hit the bottom and gradually it settled back on to an even keel. The temperature seemed to have dropped degrees all of a sudden and in the dark, the situation was even more frightening, particulary as she could hear ominous crunching noises coming from the windscreen, and at any moment, she expected it to give way and to be engulfed by a cascade of water. She reached across and switched on the interior light and had, for the first time, the chance to look around.

Janice was dead. It was obvious that as the car had hit the surface of the lake, she had been thrown forwards, hitting her head violently on the roof. Now, she was draped over the front passenger seat, her head extended at an unnatural angle and it didn't need an expert to see that she must have dislocated her neck. Cathy pushed her back, feeling a shudder of revulsion as her hand touched the woman's shoulder and the body fell back with a splash into the water, which was now covering the back seat.

Although she felt a tremendous temptation to open one of the windows and to try to get out straight away, Cathy knew that the sudden rush of water would be certain to overcome her. She switched on the headlights in case anyone above was looking for the car and forced herself to wait as the water level slowly rose higher. The fine spray coming through the windscreen was increasing in force with every passing minute and she started to take steady deep breaths. Although each movement of her chest, which had been badly bruised by the safety belt, produced stabs of pain, she forced herself to continue until she began to feel light-headed.

When the water reached her neck, Cathy knelt up on the seat, which gave her a minute or two's respite, and then, after one last breath, she sank below the surface and operated the catch on the door. The whole frame of the car must have been distorted, because however hard she tried, it wouldn't shift. She had a moment of utter panic, but then she pulled herself together and wound down the window, easing herself out. Something floated by near her head and more as a reflex than anything else, she grabbed hold of it. A moment later, she came free, kicked out with her legs and began to shoot upwards.

Cathy's feelings as her head broke the

surface were indescribable and she lay on her back for a moment, gazing at the clear blue sky and sucking in great draughts of fresh air.

'Are you O.K.?'

A young man was treading water only six feet from her and she nodded her head.

'What about your friend?'

'Friend? My friend?'

For a moment Cathy looked at him stupidly, then choked, trying to suppress the laughter which was welling up inside her and threatening to break loose.

'Come on, it's all over now. Just lie on your back and I'll give you a tow.'

# 10

Forty-five minutes later, Cathy was sitting in an office in the local police station, wearing a borrowed dressing-gown and sipping a large mug of hot, sweet tea. She was quite certain that she had broken a rib in the crash; every time she took a deep breath, a knife-like pain went through her side and to make matters worse, her burns were stinging abominably.

There were a number of occasions during the next few minutes when she was sorely tempted to pick up the phone and leave the finding of Mark Livingstone to Jim Gould, but deep down, she knew perfectly well that she was going to see it through if at all possible. It was obvious that wide publicity would be the worst possible thing for the family and if only she could get on to the baby's trail quickly, she might be able to prevent it. She had been so shaken by the events in the car that she couldn't remember in detail what Janice had said, but she had certainly given the impression that Mark was still unharmed and was being looked after by someone else.

The only immediate source of clues was Janice's handbag and she emptied the sodden contents on the table and quickly sorted them out. The results were not very encouraging; the comb, lipstick, powder compact, bottle of aspirin and purse, which contained only ten pounds in notes and some small change, she put on one side and turned her attention to the diary, cheque book and credit card. She went through the diary page by page and saw straight away that it would be a major task to check the various names, addresses and phone numbers; most of them were in London area and meant nothing to her at all. She threw it on one side and after glancing at the cheque book and credit card, which were in a false name, reached across the table for the bag itself. The sudden lancinating pain in her side was so acute that she let out an involuntary cry of pain, clutching her ribs to get some relief; perhaps, she thought, when the spasm was over, it was just as well that nothing had turned up, her side really was hurting abominably. Casually, she lifted the mirror out of its compartment in the lining and saw the scrap of paper resting behind it. The writing was smudged, but quite legible.

'Are you all right?' The red-faced sergeant had put his head round the door. 'We'll have your clothes back in a few minutes; I got one of the secretaries to take them round to the local dry cleaner and as a favour, they promised to deal with them straight away.'

'Thanks, that's great. Oh, sergeant,' she said as he turned to leave, 'does the telephone code 0272 mean anything to you?'

'Why yes, that's Bristol — we often have to ring headquarters there.'

'Any chance of getting this subscriber's name and address?'

'No problem.'

The sergeant was as good as his word; ten minutes later, Cathy had the address and soon after, the secretary came back with her clothes.

'They gave the skirt a quick press, but I'm afraid your blouse is still a bit crumpled and they couldn't do anything about your shoes — they're soaked through.'

Cathy picked up one of the five-pound notes. 'Is there a place near here where you could buy me some sandals?'

'Yes, just down the road.'

'Would you mind getting me a cheap pair — size five — also a roll of wide sticking plaster? And please buy something for yourself with the change.'

'No, I couldn't.'

'Go on, I'd like you to.'

Cathy decided not to make things more difficult by admitting that the money wasn't hers anyway and after a further brief show of resistance, the girl agreed to accept it.

Surely, Cathy thought, when she looked at the wall-map in one of the offices, it was too much of a coincidence for the telephone number not to be connected with the people who were looking after Mark. The police station was only fifteen miles from Bristol and although it would have been much quicker for them to have used the M4 out of London, no doubt Janice had selected this route to lessen the chances of them being picked up.

The woman had used one prison contact to get in touch with Grey and it seemed more than likely that she would have done the same to find someone to take the baby. Only a year earlier, Cathy had had some help over a case from the Governor of Holloway and she had no hesitation in ringing her. She got through without difficulty and explained the situation briefly.

'Was there anyone with you by the name of Wilson at the same time as Janice Beaton?'

'Yes, a young girl called Sandra, but I never heard that she was particularly friendly with Janice. She was in for six months for theft; she took some money from a till to pay for drugs — it was her second offence. She was rather a pathetic person really, nice but weak. She was in the prison hospital for quite some time; she got very depressed after

249

a miscarriage and then there was also the problem of drug withdrawal.'

'Do you know what happened to her?'

'No, we put her in touch with a social worker when she was released, but she failed to keep the appointment.'

Cathy thanked her and rang off, the pain from her ribs and the burns quite forgotten. She looked at the wall-clock and could scarcely believe that it was still only early afternoon. There was only one safe way to find out if Mark was at the address in Bristol and what part Sandra Wilson was playing in the affair and that was to go there herself.

The secretary let out a gasp of horror when she saw the livid bruise down Cathy's right side and the angry looking burns, which had been rubbed raw.

'But you can't go out like that. Let me ring for a doctor.'

'No, I'm quite all right, thanks — just help me to put some of this strapping on, would you please?'

★ ★ ★

The shock when she saw the dark-haired baby sitting up in the pram in the front of the terrace house was almost more than Cathy could bear — to have gone through all she had, and for it to be the wrong child! The little boy let out a chortle of delight when he saw her and threw the teddy out of the pram and on to the ground. As Cathy bent down to retrieve it, she saw the brilliant blue eyes and the almost white hair of part of his left eyebrow where the dye had been clumsily applied. As she straightened up, her feelings of relief were so overwhelming that she was quite unable to stop the tears from running down her cheeks and she still hadn't got full control of herself by the time the young woman had come to the door in answer to her ring.

'What's up then?' she said, taking in the obvious distress of the pale young woman wearing the crumpled white blouse.

'It's just that I was so happy at seeing the baby again.'

'Are you Joe's mum, then? I thought you weren't coming back for a couple of weeks yet.'

'Perhaps I'd better explain. May I come in?'

'Yes, do. I'll just get Joe; he's been out there for quite a long time.'

When Sandra went to pick the baby out of his pram, it was immediately obvious to Cathy how devoted the girl was to Mark, and equally obvious that he felt the same way about her, gurgling with delight and putting his arms out as she approached. She kissed him and lifted him high up in the air.

'He's gorgeous — I don't know what I'm going to do without him.'

Cathy tried to explain the situation as gently as she could, but long before she had finished, Sandra broke down and sat on the sofa, sobbing and gently rocking the baby in her arms.

'Don't cry,' Cathy said, 'you haven't done anything wrong and anyone can see how well you've looked after him. I tell you what; I know Mark's father quite well and they'll be needing someone to look after him until his mother's well again. Would you like me to ask him if he would employ you? It would mean coming back to London and living in their house.'

Sandra looked up. 'Would you really? I'd love to do that, but do you think they'd want me, what with prison and all that?'

'I can't make any promises, of course, but the nanny they used to have is really too old and once Mr Livingstone sees how well you've coped with Mark, I'm sure he'll give you a trial. Now, I really must ring up London; may I use your phone?'

Cathy was unable to reach Jim Gould, but after she had left a message for him and rung off, reaction hit her quite suddenly. She manged to make it to the police car waiting up the road, but only just. The two men came to meet her and she had hardly finished explaining what had happened, before she began to shake violently.

She saw the look that the two men exchanged and tried to pull herself together. 'I'll be alright if I can just lie down for a bit — I must be here when the others arrive from London. Would one of you be able to stay with me in the house? I'm sure that that girl Sandra was telling the truth, but I'm not going to run any risk of losing that baby now.'

'Leave it to us, you've done quite enough.'

The sergeant saw her begin to sway and caught her as she fell, lifting her up easily in his arms and carrying her back into the house. Cathy was only dimly aware of the arrival of the doctor; she did make a half-hearted attempt to stop him giving her an injection but the man brushed aside her objections and she soon sank into dreamless oblivion.

She woke up two hours later, feeling light-headed, but quite calm and by the time the car arrived from London, she was herself again. Her meeting with John Livingstone was as awkward as she knew it would be. All the time she was telling him what had happened, she could see how embarrassed and ill at ease he was.

'You will look after Sandra, won't you, John? She's had a bad time and if you could see your way to employing her, I think it would be the making of her.'

'Of course.' He hesitated for a moment, then got up from the chair by the bed. 'One of these days, I'm going to be able to find the right words to thank you properly.'

'You already have — I heard what you said to me last night and it was lovely.'

He bent down, kissed her lightly on the forehead and walked slowly across the room, pausing at the door.

'I meant every single word.'

★   ★   ★

Commander Kershaw was in a thoroughly bad mood as he came stumping up the corridor, but he just managed to raise a smile when he saw Cathy approaching.

'How did it go, sir?'

'Terrible. I hate these enquiries about as much as I hate corruption and when it's one of our own people . . . ' He shook his head dolefully. 'How are you getting on with that kidnapping business? I didn't see anything about it in the press and I haven't had a chance to catch up on the reports yet.'

'I'm glad to say that the baby was found and we managed to recover practically all the ransom money that was paid out. Luckily, too, we were able to keep the whole thing quiet.'

'You'll let me have all the details, won't you?'

'Yes, sir. Jim Gould and I have just taken our reports through to your secretary.'

'Good. You seem to have wrapped up the whole thing very quickly. So you didn't have too much trouble with it then?'

Cathy looked at him for a long moment and in an involuntary gesture, her hand went to her side. Kershaw was suddenly struck by how pale and drawn she looked.

'It could have been worse, sir, and it did have its compensations.'

'Now what in the name of Heaven is that supposed to mean?' he said to himself as he watched her walk slowly and stiffly away.

It didn't take him long to find out and when he had finished reading the reports, he leaned back in his chair and puffed contentedly at his pipe, all his depression and disillusionment dispelled.

We do hope that you have enjoyed reading this large print book.

Did you know that all of our titles are available for purchase?

We publish a wide range of high quality large print books including:
**Romances, Mysteries, Classics**
**General Fiction**
**Non Fiction and Westerns**

Special interest titles available in large print are:
**The Little Oxford Dictionary**
**Music Book, Song Book**
**Hymn Book, Service Book**

Also available from us courtesy of Oxford University Press:
**Young Readers' Dictionary**
**(large print edition)**
**Young Readers' Thesaurus**
**(large print edition)**

For further information or a free brochure, please contact us at:
**Ulverscroft Large Print Books Ltd.,**
**The Green, Bradgate Road, Anstey,**
**Leicester, LE7 7FU, England.**
**Tel:** (00 44) **0116 236 4325**
**Fax:** (00 44) **0116 234 0205**

# MURDER IN DUPLICATE

## Peter Conway

When Jennifer Prentice, a student nurse, was found dead in a locked bathroom, Inspector Newton went to St. Aldhelm's Hospital to investigate . . . Newton finds the Matron, Miss Diana Digby Scott, unapproachable. Why was Alison Carter so disliked by Jennifer? Is Vernon Pritchard, the surgeon who was having an affair with Jennifer, telling the truth? Before Newton finds any answers, there is another death and he faces mortal danger himself.